Tales from the Rain Forest

Tales from the Rain Forest

Myths and Legends from the
Amazonian Indians of Brazil

RETOLD BY
Mercedes Dorson & Jeanne Wilmot

Foreword by Barry Lopez

THE ECCO PRESS

THE ECCO PRESS
100 West Broad Street
Hopewell, New Jersey 08525

Published simultaneously in Canada by
Penguin Books Canada Ltd., Ontario
Printed in the United States

Partial segments in "The Legend of the Yara" are from *The Golden Land* by
Harriet De Onis. Copyright © 1948 and renewed 1976 by Harriet De Onis.
Reprinted by permission of Alfred A. Knopf Inc.

Partial segments in "How the Stars Came to Be" and "Uniaí's Son and the
Guaraná" are from *Subid a Pro Céu* and *A Lenda do Guaraná* both by Maria
Cecilia Fittipaldi Vessani. Reprinted by permission of Companhia Melhora-
mentos de São Paulo.

Library of Congress Cataloging–in–Publication Data

Dorson, Mercedes.
    Tales from the rain forest : myths and legends from the Amazonian
  Indians of Brazil / told by Mercedes Dorson and Jeanne Wilmot.
        p.   cm.
    Includes bibliographical references.
    ISBN 0–88001–567–5
    1. Indians of South America–Amazon River Valley–Folklore. 2. Indian
  mythology–Amazon River Valley. 3. Legends–Amazon River Valley. I.
  Wilmot, Jeanne. II. Title.
    F2519.1.A6D67 1997
    398.2'09811–dc21   97-19791

Designed by Susanna Gilbert, the Typeworks
The text of this book is set in Nofret

9 8 7 6 5 4 3 2 1

FIRST EDITION 1997

To our children
Carolina, Lily, and Malcolm

Contents

Foreword

A traveler between continents today might still notice that beyond stalled lines of traffic and apart from the bleak walls of indifferent buildings, away from the blare of televisions on a tropical night, much of the earth remains distant, cloaked in something like the original creation. These stories, more mysterious than we might at first imagine, come to us from such a place.

Despite our difference in customs, a difference in belief, when we contemplate the people in whose minds these stories first took shape, we're aware of a transcendant kinship. We move alongside them in an unfathomable world. They share their intrigue here and their desire to know, like us, where things come from–the jaguar's power, the darkness that allows us to rest, the giant water lily with its sleeping ana-conda.

People in all human cultures offer tales similar to these, stories that turn on a sense of miracle within the natural world (a world of which we're a part, but one from which we're now so estranged we've become more acutely lonely). At the outset of the twenty–first century, we can codify many aspects of the ecology of rain forests, deserts, and prairies; but we see, also, that the natural world continues to remain what it is — unfetchable to our logics. These stories reacquaint us with this fact, and with an instinct universally human — regard for nature's metaphysical core. In various cultures this regard has grown into fear, disdain, and, even worse, indifference. Elsewhere, it has matured into respect.

The stories included in *Tales from the Rain Forest* come to us like birdsong out of the Brazilian night. In them, deep within the turn of the language, is a clarion wisdom.

— BARRY LOPEZ

Acknowledgments

We wish to thank our friend, Maria Luisa Melaragno, who tracked down references, flew up books from São Paulo, and generally provided us with a conduit to Brazil.

To Peter Muller, Professor and Chair of the Department of Geography at the University of Miami, Coral Gables, we owe our appreciation for his helpful advice and geographic insights.

And, we wish to thank, too, Celso Viana Bezerra de Menezes, Professor of Anthropology at Faculdade de Londrina, Jacqui Brownstein, Michele Perna, and Victoria McCarthy.

But it is to our editor, Judy Capodanno, of The Ecco Press who we owe a debt of gratitude for her calm perseverance, editorial precision, and tireless support and good work.

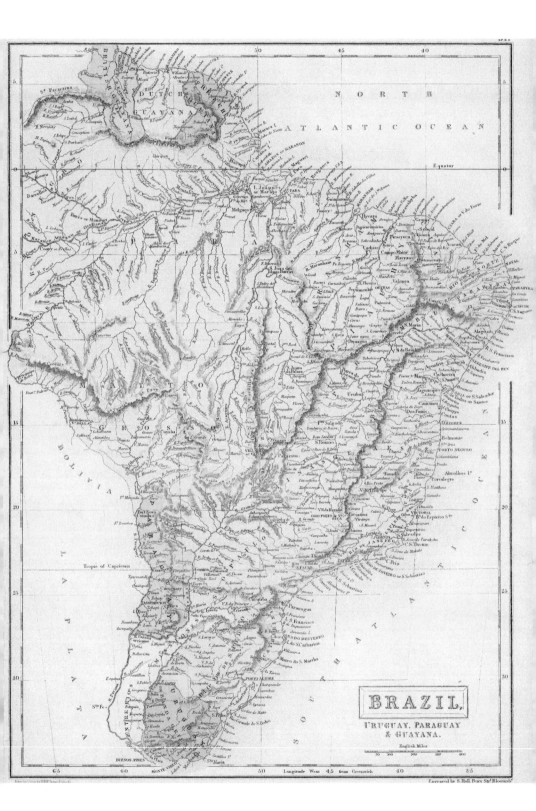

BRAZIL,

URUGUAY, PARAGUAY
& GUAYANA.

English Miles

Engraved by S. Hall, Bury St. Bloomsb.

Introduction

*In order to understand the marvelous language of
Amazonia, it is necessary to get down on the ground and
listen with compassion to the hearts beating underneath.*

—NUNO VIEIRA PEREGRINO, JR.

TERRA DE ICAMIABA

In 1541, a Spanish explorer, Francisco Orellana, set
out to chart new territory in the unknown Americas.
While traveling through South America, he came
upon a powerful river. Orellana began his journey
upstream from the mouth of the vast body of water.
He claimed he was attacked during his expedition by
a tribe of warrior women who had cut off their right
breasts to draw their bows with greater ease. Orellana recalled the Amazon women of Greek mythology, who had used the same fighting tactics, and he
named the river the Amazon. The Indians Orellana
encountered were possibly the Icamiabas, said to be
warlike women who governed their tribes in the

Amazon basin. However, because the Europeans were unfamiliar with the Indians native to this region, it is also possible the explorers mistook men for women in the denseness of the jungle and in the chaos of battle. Attuned to western culture, the Europeans associated what they saw with their own mythology. Regardless of what historical fact might be, this immense river with its hundreds of tributaries ended up with a name derived from Greek mythology.

The Amazon and its tributaries carry one-fifth of all the river water in the world and drain over two and a half million square miles of land before the main river flows into the Atlantic Ocean. The area these waters run through is called the Amazon basin and this region, also known as Amazonia, is practically all tropical rain forest.

The tales collected here are from the part of the Amazon basin located in what today is known as Brazil. The Brazilian Indians of Amazonia are the descendants of the Amerindian population that created and passed along the tales retold in this book. Originally these peoples arrived in the Americas from Asia via the Bering Strait perhaps as long as thirty-five thousand years ago. There is evidence that the

Amerindian people have populated the Amazon region for approximately half that length of time.

But the Indians are not alone in the rain forest. Over two thousand species of fresh-water fish are believed to live in Amazonian waters. The giant *pirarucu* that can weigh as much as four hundred pounds coexists with the small but deadly piranha. On land, the dense jungle, teeming with life, is home to more than thirty-five hundred species of birds, ranging from the giant macaw to the tiny humming-bird. Howler monkeys, peccaries, capybaras, ant-eaters, anacondas, jaguars, and tens of thousands of different kinds of insects find habitat in the rain forest. It has been said that the most diverse and abundant wildlife on the planet exists in this amazing part of the world. In fact, eighty percent of all species of life can be found there, and it is speculated that tens of thousands of life forms in the jungle may still be unidentified.

When European explorers first arrived in Amazonia in the 1500s, well over three million Amerindians lived in this jungled expanse. Since then, the Indian population has drastically decreased, especially during the twentieth century. In their first years of contact with the Indians, Europeans brought with them diseases that were often fatal to the indigenous population. The Indians had no resistance to Western viruses such as influenza, chicken pox, and small pox. Entire tribes were decimated by disease epidemics.

As the European colonization grew, many Indians were enslaved by the settlers and made to work on farms and plantations. By the nineteenth century, economic interest moved away from Indian labor and toward the pursuit of Indian land. Land developers began burning down the rain forest in the late twentieth century to create more grazing land and larger farms. Indian tribes which had lived in isolation for thousands of years were torn from their original lands and resettled in areas unfamiliar to them. Minerals and other riches known to exist under the Indian lands became sought-after commodities, and mines were built to acquire as many resources as possible. Greed led to the destruction of so much land that many Indians were displaced or died and currently there are only an estimated fifty thousand Indians left in Brazilian Amazonia.

For the most part, the lifestyle of today's Indians is similar to the one of their ancestors at the time the Europeans first landed in the New World. Although tribes often live in community dwellings or *malocas*, where several families occupy one large hut-like structure, it is also common for Indians to live in small, individual family houses. Males and females sometimes live separately, with the men in isolated housing. In general, all the houses are built with materials that are readily available from the surrounding area such as palm fronds, logs, thatch, and mud. The Indians hunt for peccaries, birds, monkeys, and tapirs with poison arrows and blowguns. Fish are caught by spear and bow and arrow. Most of the Amazon tribes are semi–nomadic and they cultivate new plots of land with each move. When they settle in a new site, the Indians cut down a small part of the forest, burn it, and plant crops of manioc, maize, and sweet potato in the newly cleared fields. After a few years, before the soil is depleted, the Indians shift location to allow the soil to replenish itself.

The Amerindian people live in harmony with nature and throughout hundreds of years they have not adulterated the landscape or endangered plants or wildlife. The Indians hunt and fish for survival only. The tales that follow exhibit this desire to protect the environment, and illustrate the Indians' respect for nature.

Wrapped in mystery and inexplicable phenomena, Amazonia is a region of constant fascination. The magnitude of its waters, the density of its forest, and the variety and extent of its wildlife have given birth to stories generated by the Indians' recognition of the enormous and incomprehensible forces hidden in nature. Myths are often created to explain the ways of the world, and, specifically the world surrounding a certain people. Through these tales the Amazonians attempt to interpret their world and tame their uncertainty and fears of what often seems inexplicable.

The narrative driving a myth is set apart from other stories by the fact that it has to have a purpose. The message common to so many of the tales retold in these pages is the importance of respecting the needs of the formidable jungle. Unlike in Greek mythology where gods and goddesses play paramount roles, the tales of the Brazilian Indians are dominated by animals, humans of animal ancestry, and even humans transformed into plants. Time is not linear. It is marked by the cycles of nature such as the ripening of fruit or the season of flood waters. Anything can be transformed or metamorphosized into anything else. A star can turn into a woman, a boy into a plant, a serpent can have a human daughter, and a jaguar can be more civilized than a man. The animate and inanimate are interchangeable in a way that resists logical comprehension.

Informed by the fantastic physical and psychic environment of Amazonia, the tales represent the origins of elements central to the Brazilian Indians' daily landscape. These indigenous narratives tell how different animals were created, how the night was born, and how the Indians acquired fire. They recount the origin of rain and thunder, night, the stars, plants, vegetables and other parts of the natural world. In a society where famine is familiar, food and methods of combating illness are crucial, therefore many of the myths explain the origin of special foods and medicinal herbs. To the Indians, the origin of cultivated plants such as corn and manioc is as important a theme as the origin of man.

In spite of belonging to different tribes and cultural groups, and speaking different languages, the Amazon Indians share a common philosophical outlook and similar customs. Most tribes have a shaman who serves as an intermediary between the people and the spirit world. The shaman may also be a healer, a counselor, a prophet, or the embodiment of the tribe's tradition and collective memory. As the link to the ancestors, the shaman often uses myth as a way to guide people in and out of the spirit world. The myths are spoken, not written, so it is the oral tradition that keeps the stories alive.

Although each tribe may have only one official storyteller, usually the chieftain, all the Indians partake of the act of storytelling. To enact the stories, the Indians make use of pantomime, repetition, and mimicry. They are especially skilled at the reproduction of realistic animal sounds. The telling of a story can last for hours. And, as the Brazilian anthropologist Orlando Villas Bôas said, "There are as many ways to tell a story as there are people to tell it."

Since in Amerindian culture each generation has a duty to be the "keeper of the spoken word," the material we had available through library research was abundant. When collecting the stories for this volume we concentrated on myths of origin. Our intention was not to be comprehensive, but rather to present those origin myths of the Brazilian Amazon basin that would be most evocative for a young audience. To that end, we adapted the lore presuming the literary notion that the creation of a coherent narrative would capture the imaginations of young readers.

Because the legends were originally passed down through the oral tradition, in the process of retelling these tales, we employed language, syntax, and

punctuation to replace what was normally communicated with gestures and facial expressions. Where the narrative became confusing or disjointed, we supplied connective tissue to further the cause of a structured storyline. To accomplish this transformation, we looked to ethnographies and anthropological data for first-hand knowledge. A complete bibliography is appended to this volume on page 130 and each story is acknowledged with its own list of references on page 122.

We hope that these stories will provide young people from around the world with some experience of the natural wealth of the Amazonian environment through the lens of the Indians' collective unconscious.

—Mercedes Dorson and Jeanne Wilmot

Tales from the
Rain Forest

The First
People

Long, long ago, during celestial times when the spirits
lived in the skies and the ancestors of the Indians inhabited the world of darkness under the earth, there
were two sorcerers, Aroteh and Tovapod. They lived
on the earth where together they shared a hut by a
clearing in which maize, sweet potatoes, papayas, and
peanuts were as plentiful as cassava, guava, wild
game, and land tortoises. The plants grew naturally
and abundantly so daily, Aroteh and Tovapod husked
the corn and shelled the peanuts in order to maintain
an ample supply. The corn was kept in small mounds
around the hut and the peanuts were held in dried

calabash gourds. Aroteh and Tovapod ate well and had each other for company.

One day, Aroteh noticed that the harvest was being depleted. He spoke to Tovapod about the problem and suggested that they lie in wait to ambush the thief. That night they took turns watching so that one could sleep while the other guarded the corn near the hut. Tovapod crouched patiently under the shadow of a jacaranda tree as dawn neared. He did not want to be seen circling the periphery of the hut. Suddenly he heard movement near him. Watching for the pillager, he was astonished to see an arm reaching up behind one of the calabashes. When a beautiful woman rose out of the steamy first light of the morning, she was so striking, Tovapod believed he was seeing perfection for the first time. She calmly moved over to the nearest mound of corn, but when she heard Tovapod shifting his weight, she stood still. Tovapod did not move. Since she heard nothing further, she returned to the business of gathering corn and guava. Then, as suddenly as she had materialized, she disappeared.

After a few moments Tovapod carefully approached the area where the mysterious woman had been. Nearing the very spot, he discovered an even more remarkable occurrence: human arms were reaching out

through a small hole in the earth. He thought that probably only very small people could pass through the hole
because there was an immense boulder closing off an
opening to what appeared to be a subterranean world.

The arms drew back when Tovapod kneeled to try
to enlarge the opening. He dug and dug but to no
avail. The boulder settled more firmly over the hole.
Finally he ran in to awaken Aroteh. Tovapod told
Aroteh about the world they never knew existed. He
asked Aroteh to speak to the Wind for help. Tovapod
wanted the Wind to gather her strength and blow
against his back so he would have the power to push
the boulder out of the way.

The Wind agreed to blow against Tovapod's back,
so on the first attempt Tovapod and Aroteh were easily able to shove the boulder away from the hole. The
sorcerers were amazed by what they saw. Beneath the
earth lived hundreds of people with fingers webbed
together like ducks' feet, protruding chins and horns
all over the sides and tops of their heads, long noses,
and sharp teeth. Some were ugly, some had tails, and
some looked more like animals than people.

Aroteh called to the people to hurry out through
the opening while Tovapod supported the weight of
the heavy boulder. The Wind remained at Tovapod's

back as a silent partner. Time passed and hundreds of people poured out of the crevasse. But the commotion mounted as many of them, clutching their possessions, rushed to leave the darkness.

Aroteh wondered who the people were and how they survived below the earth. They had been suffering from great hunger for many generations. All that the people had available to eat were wretched palm fruits. Then one night, one of them discovered the hole in the earth. The beautiful woman and some of the children were the only ones slender enough to pass through the opening. Night after night, they would forage for the others, bringing back armloads of cassava, yams, and bananas before the day's early light, when they would return below to their hungry friends and families.

The people had been deprived for so long that they were now desperate. In their eagerness to enter the new world, they pushed each other out of the way as they neared the opening. The quarreling slowed them down, which worried Tovapod, for he feared he would lose control of the boulder. The boulder was weighing on him, and the Wind would lose her strength eventually. As Tovapod worried, out of the chaos the beautiful woman suddenly appeared. He

almost let go of the boulder. In the woman's haste to reach the surface, however, she left something below. Tovapod tried to tell her not to return underground, but the woman could not understand his unfamiliar language. The woman started back to retrieve her possessions and was pushed into the darkness by another person seeking the new world.

The exhausted Tovapod withstood the weight of the boulder for as long as he could, but eventually he weakened. He kept searching the faces of the emerging people for the beautiful woman. She was nowhere to be seen. The Wind slowed down, and Tovapod could not manage the weight alone. He looked into the hole one last time and tried to find the woman. Still she did not reappear. Tovapod had seen that the woman had no webbing or horns anyplace on her body. She was able to move with more ease and dexterity than the rest of her people. Tovapod was disappointed to lose the woman whom he thought would be a good model for the others, but he had no choice. He had to let the boulder slide back into place and cover the hole completely.

Aroteh had already brought out straw mats for the people to rest and benches for them to sit. Tovapod's job was to shape the people's teeth, fingers, and toes because they were too sharp, and he did not want them to hurt each other. He cut off their horns and antlers, snipped off their tails, and pared down the area between their webbed fingers and toes so they could move more easily. It was a long and arduous process. Every time the sun was almost setting, Aroteh pushed it back up so that it would not get dark. They needed a long day to complete their tasks.

After everyone was fixed, Tovapod taught the people how to sing. First he taught them melody, and then he taught them language. Some people remained in the area near the original clearing, and others wandered far away where there was more space. Tovapod stretched the earth and the woods to make enough room for everyone to fit. As the people moved further and further away from each other, they separated into individual tribes and created their own languages and songs.

COMMENT: *This origin myth was adapted from tales told by the people of the Mato Grosso area in Brazil. There are various versions of this tale, and different tribes have their own myths explaining how man first came to earth. In contrast to the underground world of people in this story, some tribes of the Amazonian basin believed that the first people to populate the earth came from the sky. These tales speak of a celestial hunter in pursuit of an armadillo. When the ungainly armored animal burrowed into the hole where he lived, the hunter was forced to dig into the hole in order to capture the armadillo. Because the hunter dug too deep, suddenly he broke through the celestial vault and fell down to earth. His tribesmen could see an enormous river, palm trees, and a vast plain when they went to explore the opening in the sky. Attracted by this world that contained things new to them, they devised a plan. First they planted cotton and then with the cotton they made a long rope to climb down after the hunter. Some of the Indians did not dare follow. They preferred to remain in the sky. But it was the hunter and his tribesmen who became the first people to live on earth.*

The Creation of Night

In the beginning there was no night. Only daytime existed. There was sunshine and there were chirping birds and parrots, and mimosa flowers, and grasshoppers. But there were no crickets who sang through the dusk light nor were there night flowers like the beautiful *Victoria regia* whose petals spread at the suggestion of darkness. There was no sunset, no starlight, nor any night beasts. The jaguars, who only hunt in the night, did not yet live in the world where the people lived. The perfume of the delicate hanging orchids was burned by the bright heat of the ceaseless sunlight. There was no time to rest.

Everywhere the sun and heat urged life on with no respite.

It happened that the Great Water Serpent who lived in the depths of the Madeira River had a beautiful daughter who possessed special powers. The daughter married a handsome man from a nearby village on the banks of the river. This man worked hard preparing his field and planting manioc, corn, and sweet potatoes. It saddened the daughter's heart when she saw her husband and his tribesmen toiling in the unending heat of the sun. He was a good man, and she loved him very much. During the harvest season, he would become so tired he would fall ill. But even though he would grow tired, he could not fall asleep because there was no night.

The sun made many beautiful things too vibrant to enjoy. Even the flaming macaw feathers worn as headdresses by the men were too bright for the Serpent's daughter. She grew to hate the sparkling river water that shimmered under the power of the baking sunlight. She was enraged, for she knew that a peaceful darkness called "Night" existed at the bottom of the river where her father had taken her once. Night was inhabited by all sorts of creatures, sounds, and phenomena. The Indians had never seen Night.

Finally, she cried out to her husband, "You must send someone to my father. He will bring us Night from the bottom of the river. He took me to see it once. There are nightsongs and peace in the cool darkness there. My husband, you will be able to sleep if there is Night. A calm, dark silence covers everything where it exists."

The man protested and told his wife, "My wife, I am afraid you are delirious from lack of sleep. There is only day."

But she exclaimed, "Night does exist! Send your servants to fetch Night!" The husband had no choice but to call three of his strongest and most loyal servants.

He told them, "You must go to the Great Water Serpent's house at the end of the large river and beg him to send me Night. Tell him his daughter wishes for the peace that will come with the darkness. And his daughter desires, too, the end to this exhaustion which will cease when Night comes and we are allowed to sleep. Tell the Serpent that his daughter's happiness depends on Night's arrival. Without it she will go mad."

And so the three servants set out. They boarded a canoe and traveled downriver. They paddled past the

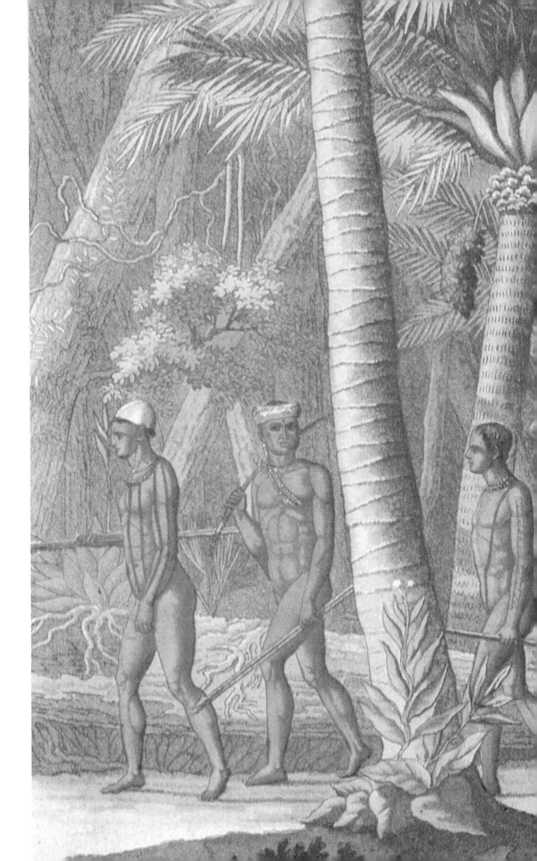

sandy cove where the crocodiles were basking in the sun and past the bend where the large fallen tree could be seen protruding from the water. Finally they found the Great Water Serpent curled up in his hammock, soundly asleep. The snake's hammock was woven from the fronds of the *miriti* palm and hung between two tall trees on the bank of the river. The men quietly tied up their canoe and slowly approached the Serpent. He was a rowdy old spirit who had just feasted on a whole tapir whose carcass lay at the foot of the hammock. A cask of *caxiri*, a rum made of manioc flour, rested against his body. With difficulty the three tribesmen awakened the Great Serpent. At the moment his ungainly body stirred, they threw themselves at his feet.

"Who are you?" asked the Serpent. "And what do you want?"

"We implore you, Great Serpent, send Night back with us for your daughter. Your son–in–law labors long and hard, and yet he can never sleep. Your daughter hides from the light of day, always shielding her eyes. She grows sadder every day, and her husband worries that she might go mad."

The Serpent drew up from his prone position and spoke in a commanding voice. "You do not need to convince the father of a suffering child to end her suffering if it's within his power to do so. Wait here until I return."

The big snake descended to the bottom of the river. He was gone for over one hour. The three servants began to worry and commenced circling the area where he had disappeared. Finally he surfaced with a large fruit from the *tucumã* tree which looked like a big brown coconut. The Serpent handed the nut to the anxious men. The men noticed that a hole had been pierced on the top of the fruit and that the hole was now sealed with hardened resin.

As the immense snake handed the nut to the nervous men he warned them, "You must not open this nut or all will be lost. If the nut is cracked, everything will become dark. Only my daughter can manage the spirits of Night. When you return to my daughter, give her the nut and she will know what must be done."

That having been said, the Serpent curled himself back up into the hammock and waved to the loyal servants who departed immediately. The three servants boarded their canoe and started paddling their way home up the powerful river.

After the servants had been rowing a while, however, they began to hear strange noises coming from within the *tucumã* nut. The servants had never before heard such strange sounds. One of the servants suggested opening the nut. At first the other two did not agree. But soon new and peculiar sounds resonated inside the *tucumã* nut. *"Shay- Shay-Shay"* and *"Tem-Tem-Tem."* These sounds were followed by a medley of nightsongs. Full of curiosity and a small measure of fear, all three servants fell upon the nut and tore at its exterior. The noises became louder, and the night calls of the frogs, the crickets, and the *murucututús* soon overwhelmed the loyal servants. Their curiosity now was stronger than they could bear. The three men paddled their canoe to the shore and lit a small fire on the muddy banks of the river to melt the resin that closed the hole in the *tucumã* nut.

As soon as the hole opened, the sky turned black. The terrified servants could not see anything in the opaque air that surrounded them until the stars emerged from the hole. Once the starlight accumulated, they were astonished by the sight of the night animals flying out of the hole and invading the darkness with their eerie sounds. A swirl of creatures, moonbeams, and dew drops blew around the servants, transforming the texture of the very air they breathed.

In her sleeping hut many forests away, the daughter turned abruptly to her husband and said, "My father has given us the gift of Night and your servants have set it free."

The toads and small frogs began to croak. The owls and snipes started hooting. The *jurutai* birds, the *acuranas*, and the bats rushed out into the darkness, filling the forest with wailings and cries and night shrieks. The imprudent servants were dumbstruck.

The husband of the Great Water Serpent's daughter was terrified when he saw the basket that lay at

the foot of his hammock transform into a jaguar with night eyes. The canoe on the river turned into a duck. The oar became a fish and the cord an anaconda. Everything in the rivers and the forest was transformed.

The man called out to his wife, "What shall we do? We must save daytime. All is lost!"

The woman pulled out a strand of her hair and told her husband, "Do not worry. With this strand I will separate Day and Night. I have no fear. Close your eyes and wait."

When the servants arrived, the husband, with closed eyes, reprimanded his men. The Great Water Serpent's daughter, who was an excellent sorceress, turned the men into monkeys for having disobeyed orders.

Meanwhile Night spun gleefully around the Water Serpent's daughter and her husband. Soon the husband fell asleep to the rhythms of the night beasts, the tree frogs, the crickets, and other night insects. Moonbeams lit the way for the newly born jaguar. Night owls hunted, and the gentle hum of bat wings comforted the daughter as she waited. She pushed aside the palm fronds at the entrance of their hut and the sweet night air her father had sent her streamed in, perfuming the darkness surrounding them. Soon, she, too, fell into a restful slumber. When she awakened, she used her strand of hair to gather up the ends of night which were scattered all over, and she forced them back into the *tucumã* nut. She picked up only part of the darkness, leaving some for people to use for sleeping and resting.

"Open your eyes, husband. Notice that dawn is coming and the birds are singing happily, announcing the arrival of the sun. And the night creatures have bedded down and are silent. The stars have disappeared into the sun's rays and the night petals of the *Victoria regia* flower are shut." From then on, Night took turns with Day so people could rest.

And so that is how Night was born.

COMMENT: *Daytime in the Amazonian jungle, under the scorching equatorial sun, can be unbearable due to the torrid heat and humidity. Nighttime brings a much needed relief from the unforgiving temperatures. Nighttime also brings some form of privacy to the Indians who often live together in communal* malocas *or houses since the only time that individuals can be alone is under the cover of darkness.*

The Water Serpent, as the father of the sorceress, illustrates the mobility between human form and animal form that is frequent in the lore of the Amerindians. The Indians do not consider themselves in a category apart from nature, and, in fact, they do not feel superior to the animals around them. In this tale, the Indians have to rely on the Water Serpent, an animal, to share the secret of Night with them.

The Origin of Rain and Thunder

In the days of the ancestors, a young Indian man named Bebgororoti went hunting with a group of men from his village. They set off at dawn and took the usual path that led them into the jungle where the best game was known to be found. After they had been in the jungle for a short while, they came across a large tapir. Together the skillful hunters killed the animal in a matter of seconds. Bebgororoti took on the task of gutting and cutting up the animal while the others watched him work. Beb-gororoti removed the entrails and went off to wash them in the river. He found a rock in the sunshine where he could lay them out to dry. While he was busy with these chores, the other hunters divided all the meat among themselves and left nothing for Bebgororoti.

When Bebgororoti returned from the river, he found that his companions had cheated him of his share of the meat. Infuriated, he asked, "Where is my portion of the game? I helped kill this tapir, and it was I who cleaned it and cut it up. I demand my share of the meat!"

"You were busy with the entrails and you can keep those as your share of the hunt," his compan-ions replied.

Indignant and raging with fury, Bebgororoti screamed at the hunters, "I insist you give me my share of the meat! I don't want the entrails. I want the meat that is rightfully mine! If you refuse to give it to me, I am leaving and will never have anything more to do with you!"

The other hunters paid no attention to Bebgoro-roti's protests. They scoffed at him and shouted, "Go ahead and leave us! We don't need you here! You should go home and wash your hands. They are still spotted with blood from the tapir!"

Bebgororoti roared at the men as he stormed away, "I will not wash my hands, I will keep them bloody!"

Thoughts of retaliation and vengeance consumed Bebgororoti. He made his way back to his village through the jungle and when he arrived home he called his wife.

"Come here," he said, "I'm going to cut your hair."

"Why?" asked the startled woman.

"Because," was his only reply.

Reluctantly, she sat down on a mat on the ground and she allowed him to cut off her long, thick hair. With a sharpened river clamshell, Bebgororoti shaved a bald triangle from the crown of her head to her temples. He called his children and cut their hair in the same way. After he had finished, Bebgororoti told his wife to cut his own hair in the same shaved triangle pattern.

Satisfied with his family's haircuts, Bebgororoti went into the woods where he gathered seeds from the *genipapo* fruit and from the *urucu* plant. He brought the seeds home where he ground them up with a pestle. The ground up *genipapo* seeds produced

a thick black liquid; and when the *urucu* seeds were crushed, the result was a bright red paste.

Confused and alarmed by Bebgororoti's bizarre actions, his wife and children watched curiously as Bebgororoti worked. They had never before seen these colored dyes and did not know what the angry Bebgororoti's intentions were. When he had crushed enough seeds, Bebgororoti dipped his fingers in the black *genipapo* juice and painted most of his body and face with black markings. Then he dipped his fingers in the red *urucu* paste and made more markings on his face and torso. After he was finished he was unrecognizable. He resembled a wild beast.

"Now," Bebgororoti said to his wife, "I need to paint you and the children in the same way that I painted myself."

"Why?" she asked.

"Because," he answered again, not giving her a reason for his behavior. He just continued to paint every member of his family to look like an animal from the jungle.

After the youngest child had been marked with the red and black dyes, Bebgororoti said to his wife, "Now I am going to leave. I am very angry. I was cheated of my share of the hunt, and I want nothing more to do with people. I am going up to the sky."

The poor woman begged him to stay, but she had no success. Bebgororoti's fury was too great. Walking out of the family's *maloca*, Bebgororoti turned to his wife and instructed her, "If you see black clouds in the sky, or if you hear a loud rumbling, stay indoors. Do not leave the *maloca*, and keep the children with you."

Bebgororoti, his face still clouded over with violent thoughts, went into the forest. He chopped down a tall *jatobá* tree and fashioned a long weapon from the sturdy wood. Bebgororoti painted the shaft of his club-sword with black *genipapo* dye, and he rubbed his hands, still bloody from the tapir's entrails and colored from the natural dyes, over the tip of his new weapon, giving it a dark red color.

Holding on to his powerful club-sword, Bebgororoti started to climb the mountain. As he climbed, his wrath increased, and he shouted curses at the men who had cheated him. The higher he climbed, the louder he shouted. The shouts sounded like they were coming from a herd of wild peccaries. The men of the village heard the cries and felt sure that there was game nearby. They rejoiced in the hunt that was about to take place.

Picking up their bows and arrows and spears, the men ran towards the animal sounds to hunt down the peccaries. As the men got closer to the foot of the mountain, Bebgororoti's shouts started to sound like rumbling and ringing, and gradually the sounds were like a rolling thunder.

It was then that Bebgororoti brandished the club-sword at his enemies. From the bloody tip of the club a flash of dazzling white fire flew out towards the astounded men. In the brightness of the lightning, the men of the village could distinguish Bebgororoti climbing further up the mountain.

"Let's kill him!" the men's leader shouted. "Arm your bows with your sharpest arrows!"

As the men readied themselves to shoot at Bebgororoti, another lightning flash came crashing down from the mountain top and made the ground tremble near them.

"Shoot your arrows!" the leader shouted again.

Arrows flew from all directions towards Bebgororoti, but to the astonishment of the men at the foot of the mountain, the arrows fell on the ground by Bebgororoti's feet, leaving him unharmed. Terrified by this unnatural show of strength, some of the men ran into the jungle to take refuge under the tall trees.

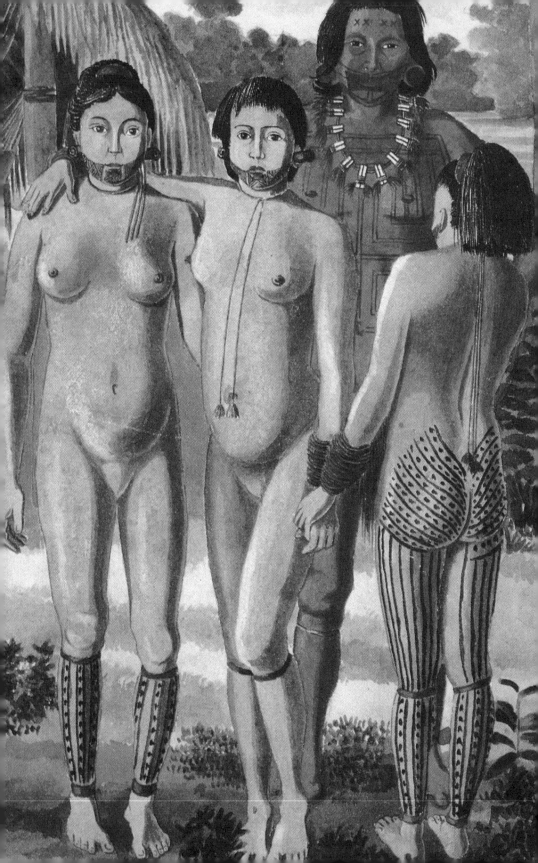

Bebgororoti's wife and children heard the wild animal noises. They recognized Bebgororoti's voice and knew that he was carrying out his plan of revenge. They stood at the entrance of their *maloca* waiting to see what would happen next. When the first flash of white light fell from Bebgororoti's club-sword, they were terrified. Forgetting his parting words, they left the shelter of their home hoping to run from the blinding crackling light.

While Bebgororoti's family ran out into the open air, the other men, spurred on by their leader, shouted insults at Bebgororoti. "We don't believe you are dangerous! You cannot harm us with your white light!"

As they continued hurling insults at him, Bebgororoti harnessed all of his strength and swung his club through the air. An immense flash of lightning, even brighter than the previous ones lit up the sky and came crashing down on the jeering men. All of Bebgororoti's enemies who stood at the foot of the mountain were killed instantly by the lightning. His wife and children, however, remained unharmed. When they looked up to the mountain they saw Bebgororoti climbing all the way up until he reached the sky where he turned into rain and thunder.

The hunters who had run for shelter in the jungle came out to look at the consequence of Bebgororoti's anger. They realized that the shaved heads and painted bodies of Bebgororoti's family had protected them from destruction.

Since that time some Indian tribes have painted their bodies with markings from the *genipapo* and *urucu* seeds. They know that Bebgororoti is up in the sky bringing dangerous lightning and thunder and rain with him wherever he goes. The Indians know also that Bebgororoti has the power to kill and to start fires. With his powerful club–sword he can send lightning and thunder down to the jungles, the plains, the villages, and the rivers.

COMMENT: *Lightning causes terror among the Indians not only because of its capacity to kill people, but also because it can cause fires. In a society where most homes are made of palm fronds and where people depend on the forest for their survival, forest fires and house fires can wreak mass destruction.*

In this tale, the first storm is created by Bebgororoti as a punishment for the injustice of men. But before ascending to the sky and transforming himself into thunder and lightning, Bebgororoti painted his body with black and red markings.

The use of body paint is very common among the Amazonian Indians, and its function varies from tribe to tribe. The geometric patterns of a tribe's body markings reappear in their weaving, pottery, and weapons. Body paint is often applied when warriors have to face their enemies, as they believe it makes them look fierce. In other tribes, it is used when storms threaten in order to ward off bad weather. Body paint can be used in festivals, ceremonies, and rites of passage. The application of body paint also has a practical aspect: the Indians have found that different clays and dyes, especially urucu, *help keep the voracious Amazonian mosquitoes away.*

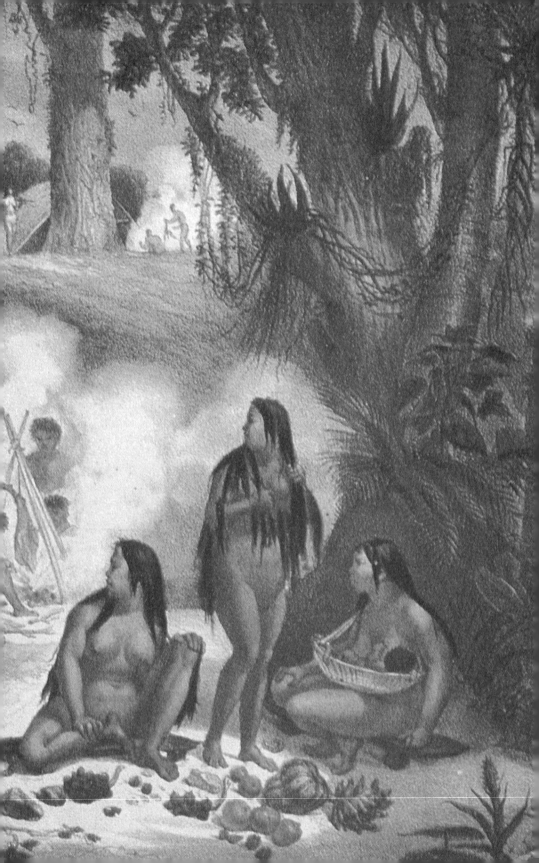

How the Stars Came To Be

There was a time when the women would periodically leave the large circle that made up their village and travel down one of the many paths that radiated out from the center like the rays of the sun. They would leave the children with the old grandmothers of the village and disappear to a strange place that was unknown to the children and men. They only took the youngest of the babies with them. When they returned to their *malocas* at night, they would come back empty-handed. The children would ask the women if they had brought anything for them in the baskets, and the women would remain silent.

Once the women would return to the tribe, the men would speak little to their wives during that night. The life of the village did not end at nighttime, and in the various intervals between sleeping and waking, the men would meet at one of the hearths and discuss the mysterious outings the women had taken. The nocturnal cover of darkness disguised the men's attempts to discover which trail the women had used to take them to their destination. Each outing seemed to utilize a different trail. While the men talked among themselves, the women would continue to remain silent, tending the fire or weaving baskets. Many of the women would rock their babies' hammocks with small strings attached to their feet so they could keep their hands free for other tasks while the babies slept. When the men would ask their wives where they had disappeared to, the women would say that they had done nothing and had found nothing.

One time when the women disappeared, leaving the children in the village to play, gather nuts, run after lizards, or make smoke to scare away the mosquitoes, a little boy who was very curious about these feminine excursions decided to take his small bow and arrows and follow the women through the jungle. He hid behind trees and under bushes as he traversed the forest trails in pursuit of the women. Although the older men of the tribe had attempted to follow the women before, they were always discovered. This boy was small and wily enough to remain undetected.

The women entered a clearing and huddled over something that held their attention. At first, the boy stayed back, but as he drew closer he could hear the rhythmic beating of the mortar and pestle. The happy laughter of the women rang through the clearing. The boy moved closer still and was able to see a large quantity of long-eared, yellow-pebbled plants on tough green stalks. There was a roasted cake of this plant and a large pot of porridge. The boy had never seen the plant before, and just as he crept up to investigate, he was caught by one of the women. Surprised to find an intruder, the woman quickly took the boy to his mother. The mother did not get angry but instead fed the boy everything they had: roasted corn, corn cakes, corn soup, and corn syrup.

The boy wondered why there was so much corn here and not a single ear of this food back at the village. It did not seem right. So after eating all that he wanted, he decided to explore further. The boy stayed to play, pretending to hunt the large lizards that ran where the corn grew wild. He roamed away from the gaze of the women and secretly went over to the middle of the cornfield. He picked some ripe ears of corn and hid the kernels in the hollow of his bamboo arrow.

On the way back to the village, the women said to the boy: "The food you have enjoyed today is called corn. Do not tell anyone what you have seen. If you keep this secret, you will always be allowed to come with us to the corn."

The boy agreed, but he asked his mother, "Why don't we have corn back in the village?"

She reminded him of his promise not to tell about the corn, and then explained to him that all the men of the tribe believed the corn to be poisonous, and they used the vegetable only as decoration in certain male tribal rites. They had forbidden it to the women and children and would not believe the women if they tried to tell them that corn was food.

Night descended upon the village, and with it came dreams of the shadow spirits who wander silently from Indian to Indian, taking the forms of birds and fish. The Indians believed that these spirits could see strange things because they traveled to unknown worlds while the Indians were asleep. When the spirits got back to their habitat, the Indians would wake up well if the dream had been a good one, and would wake up badly if the dream had been a nightmare. The morning after the boy followed the women to the clearing, the boy woke up very badly. In his nightmare he had dreamed that the men of the village discovered that he had consumed the corn. Their anger was so mighty that they secured the boy's tongue with a thin liana, or vine so he could not tell any of the other children about the corn.

The next time the women prepared to go to the forest, they wanted to take the boy with them for fear of his revealing their secret while they were gone. The boy did not want to go with the women because he believed the men would notice his absence and then want to question him upon his return. He devised a plan to trick his mother into leaving him home. The boy hid a small seed of *urucu* in his mouth which formed a red dye as he chewed it. When his mother tried to coax him into accompanying the women into the jungle, he spat out the red dye in his mouth. His mother thought he was spitting blood. Frightened, she left him in the village in the care of one of the old women.

As soon as the women were gone, the boy called some of the other children and showed them the corn that was hidden inside his arrows. He wanted the children to know about his secret.

"Look at what is available in the forest. These little yellow pebbles ripen and taste incredibly sweet."

The boy wanted the old woman to make corn porridge and corn cakes with the kernels he had smuggled home. She protested adamantly and reprimanded the boy for revealing the secret of the corn. But the boy stilled her cruelly with threats of violence and forced her to prepare the food. Once the children had their fill and the afternoon sun had begun its descent, their thoughts turned to the men returning from their day of fishing. The children worked themselves up into such a fright that they finally decided that the best place for them to hide would be in the sky.

The little boy said, "Let's make a rope. We'll tie together all our anklets, belts, bracelets, and bowstrings. Everyone go into the family *maloca* and bring back everything you find that can be tied together to make a rope."

The children came back laden with strands of

beads, belts, and bowstrings. They knotted a long, colorful rope made of brightly dyed ankle bracelets, brilliantly hued feather belts, and multicolored shell necklaces. They used bowstrings and the thick lianas to strengthen the rope and make it sturdy enough to withstand their weight.

When the rope was finished, the children called all the strongest birds to ask them if they could tie the rope to a stable part of the sky. The great blue macaw tried to fly up with the rope, but it was too heavy. The giant king vulture and the large night owl also tried. It was useless. None of the birds had the strength to carry such a heavy burden for such a distance.

The children decided to call the hummingbird, a small bird who looked weak but who could flap his wings very fast. They told the hummingbird, "Take this rope and tie it to a vine, then take the other end and secure it up in the sky."

The hummingbird did not disappoint them. He went all the way up to the sky and came back. He was so exhausted that he fainted. The children worked with small straw fans to revive the bird. They fanned him until he woke up.

Excited, the children asked, "Were you able to reach the sky? Did you tie the rope securely?"

"I did what I was asked," answered the humming-bird.

The children immediately started their ascent. First they climbed up the vine, and then up the rope that the hummingbird had tied to the end of the vine. The bigger children went first, many of them carrying the very young ones on their backs, and the smaller children followed. They looked like a line of ants running up the length of a tree trunk.

While the children climbed, the women arrived back from the clearing. They found the village strangely quiet. After a few moments they realized the children were gone. The village was deserted. The women were frantic. They searched everywhere, thinking maybe their children were playing a game and were hiding from them. One of the mothers who had started towards the jungle to look for the chil-dren noticed the rope tied to the vine. She looked up and saw the rope going into the clouds with all the children climbing up, out of sight and into the heights of the sky.

The woman called the other mothers to see this sight, and they all ran towards the jungle. Sobbing, they begged and pleaded with their children to come back down to earth, but the mothers' cries were not heeded. The children were already entering the sky. Seeing that their calls were useless, the women also started to climb up the rope. They climbed up fast, almost reaching the children. But when the last boy stepped into the sky, he took his carving tool and cut the rope.

The women fell to the earth, one on top of the other. When they fell they were all transformed. Those that fell down seated became tapirs, peccaries, and wild boars. Some others turned into pacas, agoutis, and capybaras. The women that fell on all fours became jaguars, armadillos, and anteaters. Those that fell on the trees became monkeys, hedge-hogs, and racoons. The women whose loincloths were

loose became animals with tails, and those whose loincloths were well secured became tailless animals.

The runaway children became the stars that we see shining down on us at night. And since the time the children fled their village and ascended to the sky, one can see the beauty of the sky in the faces of all the Indian children here on earth.

COMMENT: *The movement from human form to animal form and celestial bodies is seen throughout Amazonian mythology. The Indians use these transformations to explain nature, and especially the animal world.*

Pivotal to the Indians' survival in the rain forest is the preservation of the animals that coexist with them. The avowed belief of the Amazonian Indian is that wildlife is to be protected from those hunters who kill for pleasure, those who would pursue a pregnant animal, and those who destroy the young of any breed. Hunters may kill only that which is necessary for their survival.

If the laws of the forest are broken, the Indians imagine that custodial and protector spirits will appear in the shape of a white deer with fiery eyes; or as a strong Indian woman astride a wild boar; or as a young boy with green hair, green teeth, and feet turned backwards. The mission of these spirits is to preserve the species and protect the wildlife from evil hunters.

The Legend of the Yara

It is said that many years ago a young brave named Jaraguari lived on the banks of the Amazon River. This young man was as cheerful as the sun–dappled water of the great river, yet as strong and agile as the yellow–black jaguar, lord of the forest. He was the son of the chieftain of a small village. Each year, this village had a ceremony that celebrated a young man's rite of passage into the rank of warrior where manhood was honored and a boy's skills as a hunter were tested. No more exquisite a hunter than Jaraguari had ever emerged. The villagers wondered at his boldness which surpassed that of all the other

young braves who envied his courage and dexterity. None of them could approximate the uncanny precision with which he pierced the thick, hairy hide of a white–lipped peccary.

Jaraguari had in his keen eyes the strength of the great river. His disposition was as contented as the rhythmic waters that lapped along the shores of his village. The elders of the village loved Jaraguari because he treated them with kindness and respect. And the girls of the village dreamed at night of his handsome good looks, his grace, and his courage.

Paddling his canoe or *ubá* downriver with the prow barely disturbing the still waters, Jaraguari would set forth each day to fish, delighting in the skittish egrets that followed his trajectory. The river animals feared some of the Indian braves because they fished by poisoning the waters with the sap from the deadly *timbó* plants. The poison killed the *piava*, the *pintado*, and the piranha fish. But the fish appreciated that Jaraguari would not poison them. Jaraguari would use one of his sharp arrows to spear the giant *pirarucu* fish. He was nimble and elegant, and he respected the nobility of the many freshwater fish. When he returned each night at twilight, his mother would see him from shore, standing proudly in the bow of his *ubá* surveying the day's catch.

Once a young man reached the rank of warrior, he was finally able to wear a necklace made from the teeth of the jaguars he had killed in the hunt. It was several moons after Jaraguari became a warrior that his mother glimpsed him returning very late one night. The stars were already dimming in the sky. The next day Jaraguari seemed changed. He was pensive and reserved. Although his mother was concerned by his mood, he insisted on leaving that day at his usual hour, cutting the same route to Tarumã Point, where he remained until well past dusk. Each night thereafter, silent and solitary, he would return to shore, lost in his thoughts.

Astounded by the changes in her son, Jaraguari's mother finally asked him, "What sort of fishing are you doing, my son, that goes on until so late an hour? Are you not afraid of the treacherous tricks of the jungle spirits? Have you never heard voices in the angry winds? Is that why you are so sad, my son?"

His mother's words were a warning to him. When she saw Jaraguari huddled in his hammock, staring into the dead of night, hour after mournful hour, contemplating the realm of darkness, she feared what might be happening to him. Jaraguari's response to her warning was silence.

"Son, where is the happiness that animated your life? Not long ago joy danced from your eyes. Now it has traveled to a place far from you and me."

"Mother," was all Jaraguari managed to say, in a voice so pathetic he could barely be heard.

Jaraguari's mother and the chieftain watched as their son, once so fresh and full of sap, withered away. He still accompanied his father on the hunting forays, and even in his present state he did not tremble at the scream of a puma. But as a day lengthened into dusk, he would abandon the young braves still setting snares and casting their nets, and return to his canoe. With great haste he would speed through the murky waters toward Tarumã Point.

Jaraguari's mother knew that in the great river there was believed to be the Yara, or the Spirit of the Water. A woman of unusual beauty, she had light pink skin, vivid eyes, and green–gold hair falling the length of her body. The Yara tormented the souls of the men who crossed her path by slowly drawing them to her irresistible songs. Her alluring power could fill the rivers with pink and red and deep purple light. It was well known that no warrior could

withstand the Yara's enchantment. Whoever saw her was instantly attracted by her grace and charm. In fear of her power, when the sun began to set, the Indian braves stayed away from lakes and rivers where she could be found singing her eerie melodies. The unfortunate beings who were captured by her haunting incantations and beauty were dragged down to the depths of the waters.

For this reason, Jaraguari's mother stood her ground, and, though her heart was heavy with forebodings, she berated her son. "The evil water spirits have poisoned your soul. Your father and I want you to leave this village with us, and we will find a life where the bird of happiness will once again dance in your eyes."

As if witnessing a marvelous spectacle, Jaraguari suddenly came to life, his eyes wide open. "Mother, I saw her. I saw her swimming amidst the flowers, floating like the lilies in the lagoon. She is as beautiful as the moon in the clearest of skies. Mother, her hair is the color of other worlds we know nothing of, and her face is pink like the rosy spoonbill feathers dusting the sullied plain. Her eyes are like two gemstones, more fiery than the precious emerald, and her song hushes the roar of the waterfall so the river can hear her. When she looks into my eyes, I want to follow her to where the water divides and she descends to her home. There is nothing in the river a man will ever see more beautiful than the Yara. And I want to hear her song once more."

Upon hearing her son's words, the alarmed mother threw herself on the ground, sobbing, and cried out to her son, "Flee from this place, my son! Never again let your canoe reach Tarumã Point. You have seen the Yara. She is fatal. Run away, my son. Death will leap from her green eyes and kill you."

The young man did not reply. He silently walked away from the village, already enchanted.

The next day, just as the *murucututú* birds flew from their day nest on the river's edge, Jaraguari's canoe glided quietly towards Tarumã Point, cleaving the darkening water. The Indian lads fishing on the banks of the river saw him pass and cried out, "Come, everyone, come and see Jaraguari!"

The women with water jars balanced atop their heads and all the little boys chasing crabs rushed to the promontory where in the distance Jaraguari's canoe could be seen cutting through the water toward the horizon. The horizon seemed to be fed by flames from the setting sun. The nearer the canoe came to the horizon's edge, the more it appeared ready to hurl itself into the emblazoned sky.

Standing beside the young warrior was a woman of such great beauty, it was as if she were aglow herself from something luminary within. Her pale pink limbs stood out as filigree cast in relief against the blood gleam of the disappearing sun. More stunning than her beauty was the color of her long hair. As bright a green as parrot's plumage was the Yara's iridescent hair which shone like a halo of light around them both.

In the distance could be heard the screams of the braves and maidens. "It's the Yara. The Yara!" they shouted as if in one voice. They ran to the village and some could not resist looking back to see their chief-tain's son traversing the night waters of the river into the realm of darkness.

COMMENT: *Amazonian Indian villages are usually located near the banks of the numerous rivers and streams that crisscross the Amazon River basin. The rivers, lakes, and igarapés play an important part in the daily lives of the Indians. They are a source of water for drinking, cooking, and bathing. The Amazonian Indians love to swim, and the rivers and lakes are where they learn to do so from a very early age. There is an abundant supply of fish for eating in these waters, and the rivers also facilitate travel for the forest dwellers. The Indians make use of the many interconnecting rivers as a highway system on which they can paddle their canoes to other villages for trade or in times of war.*

"The Legend of the Yara" reflects the Indians' inherent respect for the waters and fear of the unknown forces encountered on the waterways. During the rainy season, the rivers can run out of control, dragging with them, in their turbulent, muddy currents, entire tracts of land and enormous uprooted trees. Even when the rivers are violent and frightening, the Indians still have to depend on them for their survival.

Uniaí's Son and the Guaraná

It is said that in the beginning there were three sib-lings, two brothers and a sister. The brothers were strong and handsome, and their agile bodies were skillfully decorated with designs made from both the red dye of the *urucu* seed and the black dye of the *genipapo* seed. The sister's name was Uniaí.

Uniaí was a tall, black-haired woman who owned an enchanted place named Noçoquém. The giant trees, all the jungle animals, and exotic plants coexisted happily in this place. Its beauty was beyond compare. Uniaí knew the secrets of the forest. She understood that the manioc root, the sweet potato, and the *pupunha* nut were for eating. She was aware that certain lianas that hung on the biggest trees could be made into the deadly poison *curare*. She knew coconuts and calabashes made the best drinking vessels and that intricate necklaces could be fashioned from the seeds of the *açaí* palm tree. Everything the brothers needed, Uniaí could provide from the surrounding jungle.

Uniaí did not have a husband. In those days animals were also people, and they all wanted to marry her. Uniaí's brothers did not want their sister to marry. They wanted her to stay with them forever, taking care of all their selfish demands. It was she who prepared the pancakes made from the manioc root to eat with the fish they caught in the river. It was she who wove the beautiful baskets out of palm leaves in which they stored the berries they collected. It was her nimble fingers that plucked the colorful feathers from the toucan to make the adornments the brothers wore on feast days. And it was Uniaí who planted the majestic nutmeat tree that dominated Noçoquém.

The snake was the first to express his interest in capturing the love of Uniaí. Every day he sprinkled a magic perfume in the path of Uniaí. If someone made a wish in the presence of the enchanted perfume, the wish would come true. Whenever Uniaí crossed the path she would exclaim, "What a lovely scent there is here!"

Each day, the little snake maneuvered himself closer to Uniaí to attract her attention. Finally, one day he stretched himself out in the middle of the path. When Uniaí stopped to bask in the wonderful scent of the sweet perfume, the snake looked straight into her eyes. He wished that she were his wife, and at that moment she became instantly married to the snake and heavy with child.

Her brothers did not like this new state of affairs at all. "Now she will only take care of the child and will not do anything for us!"

They were furious! They refused to see their sister, and once she had the baby, they refused to see her newborn son. Saddened, Uniaí left Noçoquém.

During this time, Uniaí's majestic nut tree was growing. Its limbs spread so far, it appeared to be a mass of green sky. From the tree's branches hung fruits with delicious nuts hidden inside.

Uniaí built her house far away, next to the Tapajós River. Her child was born strong and beautiful. She would bathe him in the midst of the bright blue and black morpho butterflies that hovered near the water like multicolored clouds. The boy grew taller and more handsome every day.

Uniaí would tell him stories of Noçoquém. She would tell him of the plants that grew there, of the sweet nectar from the *miriti* palm tree, of his uncles' great skill when they fished for the giant *pirarucu* fish, and of the special tree and its nutmeats.

As soon as he learned how to speak, the boy expressed his wish: "I would also like to eat the nuts. I want to taste the fruit that my uncles like so much."

"It is difficult, my son," replied Uniaí. "Now your uncles are the keepers of Noçoquém, and we cannot enter."

The boy nonetheless continued begging for the nuts that were so good to eat. His mother warned him, "It is dangerous, my son. Your uncles have placed a macaw, a parakeet, and an armadillo, whose bony-plated skin is like an armor, as guards in Noçoquém."

The boy did not relent. He insisted, "But I still want to go."

He wanted to go because he wanted to go. Uniaí knew there was no way to deter him, so she finally accompanied him to Noçoquém rather than risk his going alone. With her special knowledge of Noçoquém, Uniaí was able to sneak around the guards. The boy was so taken by the sweet fragrance of the nuts that he did not want to wait to eat them. His mother agreed to roast them right there under the tremendous tree, despite the danger of getting caught by the armadillo.

It happened that the armadillo, walking through Noçoquém later that day, saw the ashes of the fire under the tree where Uniaí and her son had roasted the nutmeats. He ran to report to the brothers what he had seen. One of the brothers was doubtful. He queried his brother, "Could it be? The armadillo may be mistaken."

The parakeet also saw the ashes and came to tell the brothers. And the macaw flew in later and confirmed the existence of the ashes as well. The brothers decided to send the fierce purple-mouthed howler monkey to guard the nut tree. They suspected that Uniaí and her son were the intruders, and they instructed the monkey to capture any creature that might appear.

The day after Uniaí took her son to Noçoquém, the boy decided to return to the enchanted place because he could not resist the delectable nuts. He knew his mother would not want him to return, so he went by himself.

The monkey saw the boy climb up the nutmeat tree. Well-hidden from the boy by the other trees, the monkey armed his bow. He shot arrows with razor-sharp edges carved out of fish bones. Many nuts fell to the ground, and the boy fell with them.

When night descended and Uniaí realized that her son was missing, she ran to Noçoquém. She ran as fast as she could. Uniaí found her son lifeless under the majestic tree. She tried to breathe life back into him, but to no avail.

Giant armadillo. *Lydekker*

She cried so hard she could not stop. She was inconsolable. In her despair she threw herself on her son. As she lay over his body, a lightning bolt struck next to them, followed immediately by an explosion of thunder. Uniaí took this to be a sign.

With new strength she spoke to her inanimate son. "Your uncles are responsible. They wanted you like this. Without life. But it will not be! From you I will make the seed of the most powerful plant ever to be seen!" As Uniaí planted the body of her child in the earth she sang:

> *"Large you will be, healer of men!*
> *All will have to appeal to you*
> *to put an end to illness,*
> *to have strength in war,*
> *to have strength in love.*
> *Large you will be."*

She willed that from the boy's eyes the *guaraná* plant would be born. The fruit of the *guaraná* plant would look exactly like the human eye. The outer shell of the fruit would resemble the eyelids. When the fruit ripened, it would reveal a large black seed surrounded by the white flesh of the fruit.

Days afterward, when Uniaí went to see the plant she had created from the pain of her son's death, she was astonished by how much the fruit of the *guaraná* reminded her of her lost son's eyes. She wanted to cry again, missing her boy, when suddenly she saw her son hidden behind the dense leaves of the *guaraná*. He looked happy, strong, and beautiful. She was gratified that her strength and persistence was matched by her son's, and that he had been born twice, once of her and now of the *guaraná*.

Uniaí's reborn son would originate the Maué tribe. It would be the Maué Indians who would discover the stimulant qualities of the *guaraná*: vigor and persistence. The seeds of this powerful plant would be used to make the tonic that gives these Indians the strength in love and war that they are known for throughout the Amazon region.

COMMENT: *The* guaraná *shrub (Paulinia sorbilis) is an essential crop for many Amerindian tribes in Amazonia. As described in the tale, the seeds of the* guaraná *have an unusual appearance and resemble the human eye. When ripe, the pink outer shell, or "eyelid," of the seed opens up to reveal a black center, the "pupil," surrounded by pulpy white fruit, the "eyeball." The roasted seeds of the* guaraná *fruit are known for having remedial and restorative qualities. The seeds are ground into a fine powder and diluted in water to make a solution that the Indians drink as an alternative to coffee or maté tea which is consumed in other parts of Brazil. Guaraná is used primarily as a stimulant, its effect due to a high caffeine content. Many Indians believe that guaraná has countless other therapeutic qualities as well. Guaraná is believed to be a panacea for a number of ailments from fevers and aches to impotence and stomach disorders.*

The Victoria Regia

There was a night, very long ago, when the old Indian chief of a village on the banks of the Madeira River told the children tales about their tribe. While smoking his pipe, he told them the stories of how their ancestors first learned about the fire and about how night was made. As the Indian chief spoke, the children glanced up to the sky. They were charmed by the necklace of silver filigree created by the moon and the stars, all shining like diamonds. The moon lit up the pink corolla of the giant water lily, known as the *Victoria regia* which floats serenely on the ponds and lakes. When one of the children asked the chief–

tain about the origin of the shining stars, the old man's eyes smiled and he replied:

"Before I tell you about the stars, you should all know about the Moon and the *Victoria regia*. The Moon is a strong and handsome warrior, and on moonlit evenings he descends to earth to meet a maiden he might marry. Many of the stars in the skies are Indian maidens who married the Moon. The star you see over there is Nacaíra, the fairest maiden of the Maué tribe. The one next to her is Janã, the most graceful woman of the Aruaques people. Now, I am going to tell you a story which happened in our tribe long ago, so pay attention.

"Among our people there was a beautiful young maiden named Naía. Naía was the daughter of the chieftain and had always heard that the Moon was a powerful warrior and a compelling suitor. She imagined that one day she would be with someone so heroic. Her thoughts returned to the Moon so frequently and with such intensity, it came to be that she was seduced by her own image of this handsome hero. Her love for the Moon was such that she did not notice even the bravest and most handsome youths of our tribe. When these young men asked to marry her, she declined their offers, believing that one day she would be the Moon's bride.

"Soon, it was Naía's routine to go into the forest nightly and gaze at the Moon, drawn to the shiny silver beams. She would run through the dense green jungle trying to reach him with her arms. Night after night she returned to the places where it appeared the Moon had touched down. She would start at twilight, chasing the Moon over rises in the forest landscape and around heavily wooded corners on the banks of the river. Always the moonlight would disappear over a hill or behind the trees. Her frustration mounted as her obsession grew. She started to sing to the Moon, asking him where she might find him, why he did not woo her. To her disappointment, the

Moon remained aloof and indifferent. In spite of Naía's great beauty and youth, the Moon seemed not at all moved by her infatuation.

"The people of the village believed she was hypnotized by the Moon. She seemed at times to have lost her mind, exploring every precipice in the forest until dawn. She did not even notice the lianas hanging down from the tall branches when they scraped her face and shoulders, or the exposed roots she stumbled over in her growing madness. Relentlessly, she tried to reach the Moon. Her singing became delirious. Her beauty was hidden by the ugly scratches that covered her once flawless skin.

"The most knowledgeable shamans from all the surrounding tribes offered potions distilled from various secret herbs. Naía's stern father, the village chieftain, ordered her to take the potions and listen to the shamans' advice. They applied poultices made from crushed roots to her forehead and cheeks. The chieftain delivered an admonition to his daughter, telling her to abandon her passion, and then he arranged for rites to be performed by the entire village. The villagers chanted these rites and circled Naía's hammock to try to rid her of her dementia. But nothing changed Naía's mind. She became so re-

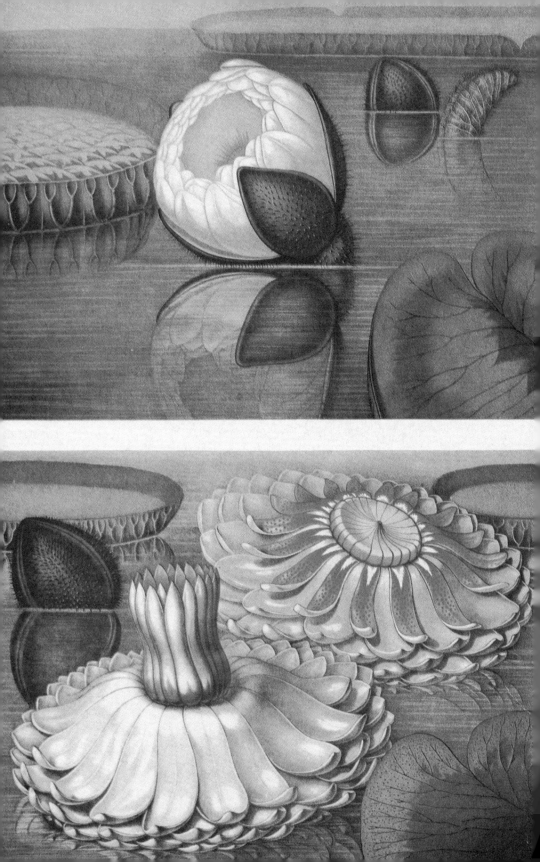

moved from her family and the other villagers that finally one morning she wandered far into the wilderness and never returned home.

"She reached the shore of a lake she had never seen before. Quite mad, yet singing joyously to the white warrior she so loved, she gazed across the water and suddenly stopped breathing. Could it be? She saw the Moon. Finally. Straight ahead. Listing back and forth softly in the water. Naía was over-joyed. She leapt forward and immediately threw herself into the deep waters. She could not lose him. She plunged deeper and deeper, but each time she swam closer, the Moon's form managed to elude her embrace.

"When Naía did not come back to the surface of the lake, the Moon knew that she had drowned. Naía would never discover that it was only the reflection of the Moon that she had seen and that once again the Moon had escaped her pursuit. The Moon had not wanted to make Naía a celestial star during her life, but to honor her death, he decided to immortal-ize her by turning her into a water star.

"The Moon transformed Naía's body into the first *Victoria regia*, the immense water lily that opens its enormous petals when darkness falls."

COMMENT: *Even in the Amazon rain forest, where the flora is so varied and many exotic-looking plants, trees, and flowers exist, the giant water lily, or Victoria regia, stands apart from all the other tropical plants. The Victoria regia first became known to the Europeans in 1840 when Robert Schomburgk, an explorer and botanist, encountered the enormous floating flower during an expedition to the Amazon. He named the incredible flower after the British sovereign at the time, Queen Victoria.*

The floating leaves of the Victoria regia can measure up to six feet in diameter and can easily support the weight of a coiled boa constrictor. The seeds of this aquatic plant are the size of a child's head and are ground up by the Indians to make a fine, white meal used in cooking. They call these seeds "corn of the water." The majestic, fragrant flower looks like an immense rose with huge petals that are pink on the outside and red in the center. The Victoria regia flower remains closed during the day and only opens up after the sun has set.

The Origin of Birds, Plants, and Soil Termites

A long time ago, when the Sun still lived on earth among the Indians who lived along the shores of the Tocantins River, and many of the plants and animals we know now didn't exist, there was a very old man living in the forest with his tribesmen. The old man had seen countless births and deaths among the people in his village. He had seen pestilences come and go and had suffered through droughts and rainy seasons. He had taught his sons and grandsons and their sons the art of fishing in the nearby rivers and lakes, and the skill of hunting in the impenetrable jungle. The years of hard work and hard living had taken their toll on this aged man. He was barely able to walk, and his frail body had to be held up by the younger men of the village. Most of his teeth were missing, so he was unable to chew his food. His grandchildren carefully ground up his manioc and fish into a fine paste when he wanted to eat. He was very weak.

The villagers knew that the old man would not be among them for very much longer. One day the tribe's shaman was watching the old man and noticed a faraway look in the elder's glazed eyes. The worried shaman went in search of the Sun to ask him if the old Indian was going to die soon. The Sun answered that in spite of the Indian's advanced age, he would not die.

"Why not?" asked the shaman.

"Because he has come to me and asked to be transformed," answered the Sun.

The shaman, puzzled, looked at the Sun, awaiting

further explanation, but the Sun only said, "Go and gather some of your strongest warriors. We have work to do in the forest."

The shaman and his men followed the Sun, who was holding a hollowed-out tortoise shell. They traveled through the cool, humid underbrush, past the rivulets, past the mist-covered lake, and into the densest part of the forest. The Sun chose a spot next to a tall *pequí* tree where he wanted his companions to work. The men set to their task immediately and swiftly cut down the vine-entangled giant *ficus* trees, the towering Brazil nut trees, the smaller palms with their clinging orchid plants, and the prickly bushes. Towards the end of the day, a large, round, vacant area of land stood in the midst of the thick jungle. From the center of the clearing the men were able to look straight up at the blue sky. They could see far above them without having their view blocked by the canopy of trees that usually shaded their eyes from the brightness of the day.

As he admired the clearing, the Sun told the men to go back to their village and fetch the old Indian. When they arrived with the old man, the Sun placed him in the center of the newly prepared land. The Sun ordered the shaman to cut the old man's hair and put it in the hollow tortoise shell that he had carried with him. The shaman took his cutting tool that he had fashioned from a sharpened tapir bone and cut the old man's hair, being careful not to hurt him.

"Now," said the Sun to the shaman, "take out some of the hair you cut from the old man's head and throw it up into the air. Then blow on it."

The shaman asked, "Why should I do that?"

The Sun told the shaman he must trust him and encouraged the wise man to do as he instructed.

The shaman reached into the tortoise shell that he had placed on top of a tree stump and brought up a handful of hair. He opened his hand, took a deep breath, and blew the hair strands off the palm of his hand into the still air. The shaman and the men who were gathered around him saw the hair spread out into the air and transform into large king vultures with shiny black feathers. The Indians were incredulous. As the vultures flew away, the shaman took out another bunch of hair and repeated the action. From each hair a curassow was born. These large ungainly birds immediately landed on the ground and waddled away into the forest.

"Do not stop," said the Sun, "keep blowing the hair into the air."

1. COFFEE. 2. TEA. 3. DATE-PALM. 4. BANANA. 5. CACAO. 6. JACK FRUIT. 7. BREADFRUIT.
8. PISTACHIO. 9. PANDANUS. 10. GUAVA. 11. LITCHI. 12. BRAZIL NUT. 13. MANGO.

The shaman held another handful of hair in the palm of his hand, and, when he blew on it, a flock of large, gray, ostrich–like emus appeared. The flightless fowl stood as tall as the men who watched in amazement. The birds high–stepped into the jungle on the thin, strong legs that so efficiently supported their heavy bodies. The shaman continued his task, and as he blew on another lock of hair, all the macaws and parrots flew out into the sky in a flamboyant display of color. The scarlet and green macaws took off first, followed by the macaws that were blue and yellow, then, finally, the all–green parrots ascended. Next came the multicolored toucans with their large painted beaks, croaking loudly as they flapped their heavy wings.

The shaman continued until all the other large birds that exist in the world came into being, among them, the snow–white egrets with their long legs, the scarlet ibis, and the rosy spoonbills. They filled the sky and the surrounding forest with their radiant colors and melodious songs.

After the large pelican was born, the Sun said to the shaman, "Now gather in your hands all the thin hairs that are left in the bottom of the tortoise shell, and with one strong breath, blow them all up into the air at once." The shaman obeyed and the small birds were born. The air sparkled with the glitter of the jewel-like hummingbirds, the brilliance of the cobalt-winged parakeets, and the shimmer of the gaudily plumaged manakins. The birds that were meant to fly soared up into the trees as soon as they were born. The ones that were meant to walk remained on the ground.

While the Indians stood in the clearing transfixed by the colorful spectacle provided by the birds as they gracefully flew from the top of one tree to another, the shaman asked the Sun what was to be done with the old Indian.

"We will make him as comfortable as possible and let the melody of the birds envelop and soothe him as he transforms yet the rest of his body for our benefit."

And that was all that needed to be said. The Sun, the shaman, and the warriors, exhausted from the toils of their day, made their way back to the village through the winding jungle path.

Meanwhile, in the middle of the clearing, the old Indian transformed into all the plants that are good for the Indians. The bones of his torso turned into an enormous and beautiful guava tree, and the dark

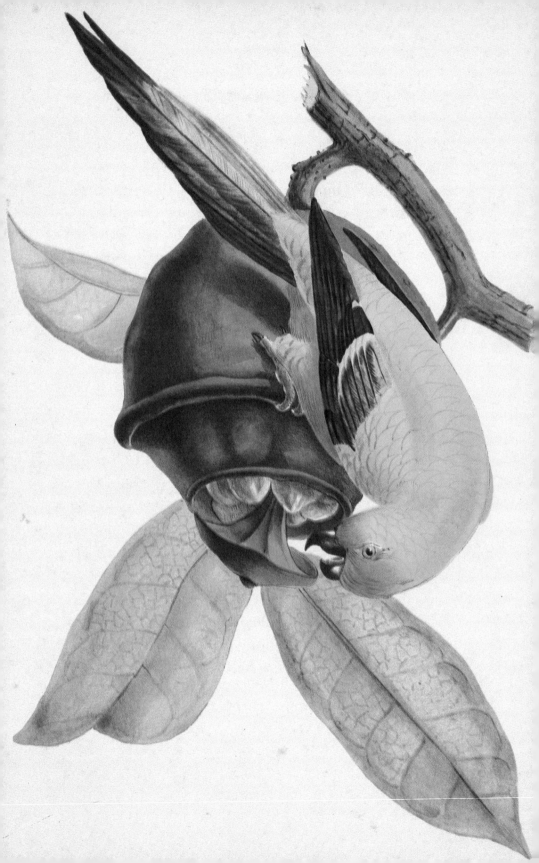

green surface spreading out from what used to be recognized as his fingers became the leaves of the tobacco plant. His ears turned into sweet potatoes, or yams, and his ribs became bananas. His fingernails became cashew nuts and his toenails kernels of corn.

A few days later, when the Indians returned to the clearing in the woods, they saw that the Sun's words had come true. As they plucked the delicious foods scattered around the ground where the old Indian had sat, they noticed that even the old man's eyelashes and eyebrows had been transformed. They had turned into the soil termites that eat the rotten branches and dead leaves that lie on the ground of the rain forest.

In this way, the old Indian from the shores of the Tocantins River exists forever, and for everyone.

COMMENT: *As in so many of the origin myths found in the Amazon Basin, transformations lie at the center of this story. The concept of transformation helps the Indians explain the natural world around them as it affects their survival.*

The final transformation in this tale, when the old man's eyebrows and eyelashes become soil termites, demonstrates the important role that soil termites play in the ecological cycle of the rain forest. By eating the rotten branches and leaves that lie on the ground of the forest, the soil termites help break down the elements that are no longer useful in the ecosystem. Once broken down, the elements convert into nutrients that are absorbed by the roots of plants, making possible the growth of luxurious vegetation in an area of poor soil.

The Brazilian Indians see themselves as part of nature. Their concern for ecology and for the maintenance of the balance of nature is elemental to their beliefs. Everything in the forest has a role to play, and nothing, no matter how small, can be taken for granted. Even the body of an elder tribesman contributes to the well-being of the forest by being transformed into birds, food, and soil termites.

The Young Man and the Star Maiden

Long ago, in the days of the ancestors, the Indian tribes did not know how to cultivate plants. They survived only on what they could hunt and gather in the forest or fish in the rivers. They did not know how to prepare a field for farming. Although the Indians had seen corn and sweet potatoes, they never considered either vegetable as food. They thought corn was poisonous and ate only rotten wood, leaves, and wild coconut with their meat and fish.

There were periods during the rainy season, when the woodlands were flooded, that the Indians suffered great hunger because they could find nothing to eat.

It was at this time that two brothers lived with their father in a village near the river where the forest was the least dense and the stars the brightest. The elder brother, Acauã, was renowned for his bravery. The number of jaguar pelts decorating his *maloca* was unsurpassed in the village. He proudly wore a necklace that commemorated the game he had killed for his tribespeople. The necklace wound multiple times around his neck, showing artfully the teeth of his prey and the perfectly paired jaguar claws.

The younger brother, Caué, was a quiet boy who loved nothing more than to watch the life of the forest unfold before him. Of a day he might spend the morning gazing at the water lilies studding the green pools lost in the shadows of the enormous *ficus* trees. Hiding in a bamboo thicket for the afternoon, the boy would follow shafts of sunlight that led him to the fiery colors of a mother manakin hovering over her nest. For hours Caué could watch the natural world demonstrate its vivid power through the wondrous details of the everyday. And, when the vi–

olet sky darkened to a mist, pierced by the silver sparkle of the first stars of night, the boy would return home to his father. The father took great pride in Acauã's accomplishments, and, although he believed Caué to be idle, he was just as pleased with the younger boy's good nature.

One evening, as was often their custom, the brothers sat with their father and listened to him recount the legends of their tribe. While they sat looking up at the star-filled sky, Caué felt a strange sensation. He was unable to take his gaze off the brightest star that shone above him. His heart started to beat very strongly, and he felt as if he had become paralyzed.

"What is it that shines so brightly up there?" he asked his father. "I would like to touch that brilliance."

"That brilliance up in the sky is the Star Maiden. She is very far from here and impossible to reach. The only way you might touch her is by wishing for her fervently. If she feels you calling and decides to come and live with you as your wife, your wish may come true."

The old man's eyes twinkled as he remembered first hearing this story from his father. He had wished and wished, but the Star Maiden had never chosen him or anyone else from his tribe.

That night as Caué tried to fall asleep, he could not keep his thoughts away from the luminous star.

But Acauã, the great hunter, whispered in his ear, "Every girl in the village makes sweet *beiju* cakes for me. And I yearn for none of them. Perhaps this Star Maiden will be my wife."

The young boy realized that his glorious brother would also endure a sleepless night filled with longing for the Star Maiden. He was certain that if the Star had to choose, she would choose the courageous Acauã whose achievements could be measured by the length of his necklace and the numbers of pelts adorning his *maloca*.

The next day, the boys went out hunting for peccaries and armadillos. They wandered far away from their village, and as the Amazonian sky started to color and the sun plummeted toward the horizon, the brothers decided to stay where they were for the night. They would return home the following morning by daylight. Settling in for their evening meal, they made a fire and cooked a small armadillo they had caught earlier. After eating all they wanted, they gathered some dry rushes on which to rest their

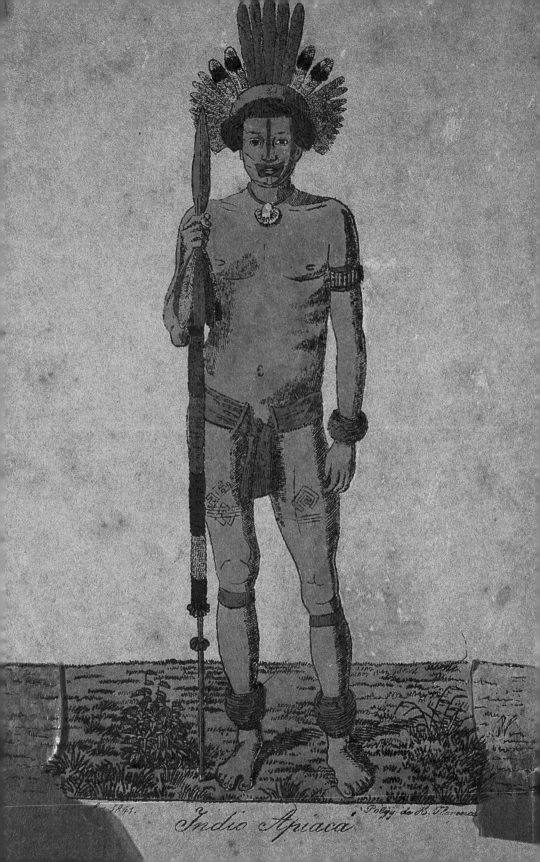

Indio Apiacá

weary bodies and laid down for the night. It was a clear, moonlit evening, and the young men admired the cover of stars shining down upon them. The beauty of the Star Maiden was as captivating this night as it had been the night before, and Acauã ardently wished that the Star would come down to earth to be his bride. Caué fell asleep alongside his brother, believing that there was no chance that the Star Maiden would ever consider him a worthy suitor.

In the middle of the night, the boys heard someone enter their clearing. Frightened, Acauã called out, "Who is there?"

"It is me, the Star Maiden," answered a voice.

Filled with excitement, the boys rushed toward the radiance they saw in the darkness. They lit a fire to have a look at the brilliant star.

They were amazed by what the firelight revealed. The star that shone so brightly in the sky was actually an old woman. Her hair was as white as cotton, and her skin was withered to a thick hide. Acauã believed he was being deceived.

Enraged, he bellowed, "Go away! I do not want you for a wife. You are too old and too ugly."

The old woman turned away from him and

started to cry very quietly. When Caué saw this, he ran up to the old woman and took her hand in his.

He said to her, "I would like to marry you. I would like you to be my wife."

The old woman brightened up and in a timid voice declared how pleased she would be to marry him. But what the boy had not considered was how the villagers would feel about the Star Maiden in their midst. The Star Maiden further explained to Caué that she could only be out during the darkness because she was a creature of the night. They agreed that, for the time being, the old woman could live in a gourd. The brothers found the largest gourd nearby from the plentiful forest and cleaned it out with the sharpened edge of a fishbone. When day-light filled the jungle, the two brothers set out for the village carrying the gourd.

When they reached their father's hut, they told him of the Star Maiden resting inside the gourd, but each boy had a different story. Acauã reprimanded his father for encouraging him to entice the Star Maiden to earth. And Caué, lingering less behind his brother than usual, interjected that his delight over the arrival of the celestial woman would stay with him forever. The father, intrigued by the new circum–

stances, asked to meet the woman who waited so patiently inside the gourd.

When Caué opened the gourd, out leapt an opossum. Acauã drew back in fear because this animal
was taboo to boys, and all were forbidden to eat its
meat. The creature jumped onto the father's shoul-
der and skipped over to a large plant laden with
maize. Climbing from stalk to stalk, the opossum
threw the old man large quantities of corn. Then the
opossum transformed right before their eyes, and
the Star Maiden reassumed her human shape. The
old father, shocked by her advanced age, openly
stared at her. He comprehended that something remarkable was occurring. The father and Caué listened in earnest to the Star Maiden as she instructed
them on the making of maize cakes. Although he believed that corn was a poison, the father held his
judgement in reserve. He would not partake of the
corn cake, but his son, Caué, consumed the entire
cake. Acauã turned to leave, laughing to himself,
convinced that his brother would have a terrible
stomach pain soon enough.

The next day, Caué was as happy and healthy as
ever, and he bragged about the merits of corn cakes.
Acauã stayed away from their *maloca*, filled with a

sense of foreboding. Caué carried the gourd around with him all day and all night, and occasionally, when no one was around, he would open up the gourd to converse with the Star Maiden. By the end of the day, when it was certain that the boy would not be made ill by the corn, the Star Maiden knocked from inside the gourd and requested that she be let out to prepare his wedding gift.

"Now I have to go into the forest where I will cultivate many good things to eat. I will show you what can be done with plants you already have in your midst, and I will introduce you to new ones. But you may not accompany me. I must go alone."

There would be three stages to her gift. The first would be the seeds to the new plants that would help the villagers thrive during times of hunger. The second would be the cultivation of those seeds so the plants could continue to grow and reproduce. And the third stage would be the techniques of food preparation which would allow the Indians to enjoy their foods in various ways.

The old woman started off in the direction of the river. When she reached the bank, she stopped, said a few words of magic, and then walked into the water up to her knees. There, she leaned down, and faced the current. From time to time she would drop her hand into the water and bring up a few seeds. Holding onto the seeds, she then left the river and walked into the forest. On the second day, she cleared the land and prepared it for planting. On the third day, when the garden plot was ready, the Star Maiden went up to the sky and brought back rice, beans, and peanuts. On the fourth day, she hollowed out an oven in the ground and filled it with red–hot stones sprinkled with water. She planned to demonstrate later how to use the little oven to stew and bake food. On the fifth day, she flew back to the sky and brought back the seeds for guava, *maracujá*, and pineapple which she would teach her young man to grow.

By the sixth day, Caué worried that his wife–to–be had not returned. The woman was too old and weak for the hard labor that was required to survive for five days in the jungle. The boy thought that maybe she was hurt. As the afternoon dragged on, and the rays of the sun became longer, the youth was unable to wait any longer. He set off to find the old woman. He knew that night was rapidly approaching, and, although he was disobeying the Star Maiden's orders, he felt he must go for her.

Acauã was very mistrustful of the Star Maiden, so he arranged to have his brother followed. He gathered some friends and explained the suspicious circumstances surrounding the old woman. The group discreetly followed Caué into the forest, and Acauã remained in the village.

When Caué arrived in the area of the forest where he thought he might find the Star Maiden, he was disappointed not to see the old woman. He traversed a small trail that appeared to be created recently, and the group of boys followed behind him. The trail led from the river to an open field.

Once in the clearing, the boy was astonished by what he saw. Distinct concentric circles emanated from a center where even lines of sweet potato were planted. He was surprised to see a young woman putting the sweet potato plants into little mounds of dirt in the ground. Then he noticed the woman doing the same in another circle which contained what he later learned were beans, papaya, melons, pumpkins, yams, cotton, and tobacco. She continued in the third circle, planting what looked simply like the surrounding forest but was, in fact, banana trees. Upon finishing her work, the woman scattered warm ashes over the field. All the while, unbeknownst to the young man, Acauã's friends watched closely. As Cauê started toward the woman, the other boys ran back to the village to report to Acauã.

Cauê drew closer and saw that the woman was a beautiful young maiden with strands of starlight woven into her hair.

"Have you seen an old woman around here?" the boy asked the maiden. "She is to be my wife, and I am very worried because she hasn't returned to the village in almost six days. I am afraid something has happened to her."

"I am Star Maiden," answered the beautiful raven–haired girl. "I am not an old woman. I took on that appearance to test the feelings of your brother, who so intently wished to marry me. The experiment proved that I was right to doubt his sincerity. I am happy that you wanted to marry me in spite of my appearance. It is to thank you for your kindness that I have planted this field for your people. You will all be able to enjoy delicious vegetables and fruits that grow from the earth."

With that, she handed the young man a melon and a papaya. He cut open the melon with the edge of his spear, and tasted the succulent flesh of the fruit. While the young man savored the delectable fruit, the

Star Maiden prepared a yam to bake in her little oven. But, overjoyed by the incredible new world of food available to his tribespeople, the young man took his lovely Star Maiden into his arms and excitedly started toward the village. He could not wait to tell his people of the great bounty the Star Maiden had bestowed upon them. They planned to marry and celebrate their great love, and then the Star Maiden would complete the final stage of her gift and teach all the villagers how to prepare the new foods.

But when the couple reached the village, the boy's *maloca* had been burned to the ground and his father sat alone outside, weeping silently at the destruction. Acauã had told the rest of the young braves about the opossum and the corn cakes. After hearing the story, some of the youths in the village decided they would discover the secret of the gourd for themselves. They waited for the time when the boys and their father usually went to the river to bathe, but when they entered the hut, they were surprised to find the father protecting the gourd. They wrenched the gourd from his safekeeping, destroyed it, and proceeded to set the hut ablaze. The squashed gourd lay at the father's feet next to his bow and arrows and fishing hooks.

Caué and his beautiful and powerful maiden were filled with rage and sadness. The young maiden turned to the two people who would become her new family and said, "Come, my friends, with me to the land of the stars. There, no angry and fearful tribespeople will hurt you. Even greater bounty flourishes in my world, and all the gifts I would have given to you here I will instead give to you there."

And with those words the Star Maiden took her beloved and his father, and they set forth immediately on their long journey to the land of the stars. And it is because of the mistrust and fear of the tribespeople that the Indians on earth do not have all the wonderful things that exist in the celestial world.

COMMENT: *When it comes to cultivation, many Indian tribes have a complex system of plant-animal management and conservation. Planting time is based on lunar phases, as it is believed that destructive mammals and insect pests are least active during moonlit evenings. As described in the story of the Star Maiden, the planting is done according to a determined pattern. The concentric circles that make up a Cayapo Indian plot, for instance, are each meant for a different group of crops. The center area, where the soil is frequently aerated* and enriched with ash and organic matter, is reserved for sweet potato and taro. A second circle is reserved for more nutrient-demanding crops such as beans, papayas, and melons. The Cayapo Indians know how to combine dozens of plants to create ombiqwa otoro which means "friends that grow up together." They have learned that certain plants secrete poisons underground to keep neighboring plants at bay and that other species grow better at close quarters.

In addition to basing their planting seasons on lunar phases, the Indians of the Amazon Basin practice biological pest control. They surround their gardens with a buffer zone that contains banana trees which lure wasps. The wasps then kill the caterpillars and other leaf-eating insects which destroy the valuable crops in the inner circles.

Instead of concentrating on single-species plantations, the Indians practice biological diversity. They have had time to discover countless uses for the natural resources around them and have learned how to manage them and grow them successfully.

Botoque, the Jaguar, and the Fire

One day, an Indian went out to hunt for baby parrots with one of the youths of his tribe named Botoque. After a long walk, the Indian noticed a macaw nest on top of a tall and narrow cliff. When the Indian saw two red-billed macaw parents fly off to find food for their nestlings, he convinced Botoque that he should attempt to capture the young birds left behind in the nest. The Indian leaned a long pole against a rock so the youth could climb up to the nest. Once Botoque reached the nest, he saw not only several baby birds but two eggs as well.

Botoque tossed the first egg to the Indian, but as it fell through the air, it changed into a stone. Neither noticed that the egg had become a stone until it reached the ground. The Indian stared at the stone at his feet and looked up at the startled youth.

"Throw the other egg down," the Indian ordered.

This time, Botoque carefully tossed the second egg, but again it transformed into a white stone in front of his eyes. This stone wounded the hand of the surprised Indian below and he angrily blamed Botoque for his injury.

Furious because he believed he had been fooled, the Indian broke the pole and left Botoque atop the rocky cliff. Botoque screamed after him in fear and held up the baby birds from the nest.

He called out, "Here are the little ones! Come back! This must be an enchanted nest! Those stones were eggs."

The Indian did not turn back to see what happened next, but if he had, he would have seen the pair of adult red-billed macaws return. When the parents discovered what Botoque had done to their nest, they screamed fiercely. With this, the nestlings suddenly turned into mature birds. They flew up to meet their parents, and all four birds disappeared into the flaming sunset.

Botoque remained abandoned on top of the huge rock for several days. He saw no one and spoke not at all. Botoque became so hungry and thirsty that he ate what was left of the nest. Finally, a spotted jaguar passed by, carrying a bow and arrow and all sorts of fresh raw game. The Jaguar wore finely woven vines colored with red dye from annatto seeds, and he stood upright. His bearing and manners were more civilized than any creature Botoque had ever met. Botoque almost cried out, but he stopped himself in fear of the unfamiliar creature. The Jaguar, walking underneath the boulder, saw the boy's shadow on the ground. He wanted to catch the shadow, but it kept moving as Botoque tried to stay out of sight. The Jaguar looked up suddenly and caught a glimpse of the creature to whom the shadow belonged. In a pleasant tone, the Jaguar asked Botoque his name.

"I am Botoque. My tribesman talked me into capturing some birds for him, but then he left me stranded."

The Jaguar laughed, accustomed to the macaws' enchanted ways. He felt pity for the hapless boy and helpfully offered to cut footholds in the stone so the boy could climb down.

The Jaguar was older and grandfatherly, so when he encouraged Botoque to come down, the youth started to do so. However, as Botoque drew closer to the Jaguar, he saw how big the creature was, and he became afraid. The Jaguar understood Botoque's hesitation, and he coaxed the youth in a friendly way, promising him assistance.

"Come down and climb onto my back. I will take you to my dwelling where there will be lots of grilled meats."

The youth asked what grilled meat was, since in his tribe he had only eaten meat raw or dried from the sun.

"You have a delicacy awaiting you at my home. An entire boar roasted by the fire from a burning *jatobá* tree," explained the Jaguar.

Eagerly the boy completed his descent and when he entered the Jaguar's cave, he saw fire for the first time. An enormous tree trunk was aflame and smoking and everywhere small gatherings of rocks the size of coconuts bordered pieces of tree trunk bursting with flames.

Botoque asked the Jaguar, "What are the plumes of orange dancing light near your cave?"

The Jaguar smiled and dangled a morsel of roast boar in front of Botoque, answering coyly, "Taste this, my young son. It has a tenderness you're not acquainted with and a smokiness from the fire that cooks it."

How good it tasted to the boy! Being as hungry as he was, Botoque gorged himself on the tender delicacy he had never before tasted.

Off to the side of the dancing flames stood an Indian woman whom the Jaguar introduced as his wife. Botoque knew that she took an immediate dislike to him because of the suspicious look in her eyes. She referred to him as "*Me-on-bra-tum*," or "abandoned one" and indicated to the Jaguar that the boy should not be trusted. But, despite his wife's protests, the Jaguar wanted to adopt Botoque because he liked the boy very much and the boy had already grown fond of the elderly Jaguar.

The Jaguar told his wife, "I have no children of my own, and, especially because he is abandoned, I want to share my home with Botoque."

After Botoque had eaten, he drank until he became sick. The Jaguar's wife tended to him during the night, but when she was alone with him she tried to scare the boy. She picked lice out of his hair and told him the lice would crawl all over his body if he stayed in the cave. She opened her mouth wide and bared her teeth, telling him stories of wild animals in the Jaguar's cave. The youth screamed out in terror, and the Jaguar was aroused from his sleep. He told his wife to stop tormenting the boy.

Every morning, the Jaguar went hunting, leaving his stepson with his wife. Her hatred for Botoque grew daily. When the boy asked for something to eat, the old woman gave him tough, bad-tasting meat. She scratched his face and eyebrows, pretending she was searching for lice. Things became so unpleasant for Botoque that every day he would leave the cave and flee into the woods until the Jaguar returned home.

The good Jaguar scolded his wife but since she still continued to mistreat Botoque, the Jaguar made a new bow and arrow and gave them to his stepson. The Jaguar taught Botoque how to use the weapon because he feared that his wife might harm the boy. The boy had never seen a bow and arrow before the day the old Jaguar rescued him because the Indians hunted only with spears. And, although he did not want his stepmother to continue tormenting him, Botoque was uncomfortable with the new weapon.

Finally, Botoque became so homesick for his village that he went to his stepfather and asked to return home. The old Jaguar felt saddened, but he understood. The Jaguar collected a feast of grilled meats and put them in a basket the boy could wear astride his back. He warned Botoque not to tell any of the Indians about the existence of fire, and then the Jaguar sent Botoque on his way.

Darkness lay over Botoque's old village like a mat of dense hemp. Botoque had to feel his way along the walls of the communal house to his mother's hammock. When he found her, he had a hard time convincing her that he was alive. She had missed her son so much, she had fallen into a deep grief. Now she was stunned and overjoyed. All the people of the village gathered together, and Botoque told his tale. He distributed the grilled meats for all to taste. The village was astonished as they shared the delicious cooked meats the youth had brought to them from his stepfather, the Jaguar.

When the villagers questioned Botoque about the roasted meats, he resisted revealing the Jaguar's secret of fire. Instead, he tried to distract them by demonstrating the bow and arrow. Although the Indians were intrigued, they returned to the subject of the delicious cooked meats. Finally the pressure from his family and the village elders was too much for Botoque. He told them about fire, about its magical light and great warmth. The villagers grouped together in the shaman's meeting house and after much discussion they agreed to steal the fire from the Jaguar. They devised a plan to bring the fire back with as little danger as possible.

The next day two of the Indians accompanied Botoque to the Jaguar's cave. Other Indians followed and took up stations at various locations along the way in order to relay the fire back to the village.

When the three Indians arrived at the cave, the Jaguar, as predicted, had already gone out hunting. They found no trace of the stepmother, and Botoque explained that the Jaguar probably had exiled her for her cruelty towards Botoque. The Indians marveled at the beauty and power of the dancing plumes Botoque told them was the fire. But more powerful than the beauty of the fire was its warmth. The villagers had never experienced this feeling from anything on earth. Until that moment, they had believed that only the magnificent sun in the skies could provide such a sensation.

They found the game of the hunt from the day before and Botoque saw that it was raw. He was certain that his mean stepmother had been sent away, otherwise she would have roasted the meats. The Indians were so excited, they immediately cooked the raw meat and ate it.

Once all the roasted meat was eaten, the two Indians wanted to start taking the fire back to the village. Botoque resisted again, however, he was not strong enough to withstand the arguments of the two Indians. How could he deny his mother and all the villagers warmth, cooked meats, and light to protect against the danger of darkness?

Once Botoque and the other Indians set about collecting all the burning tree trunks at each hearth, they then relayed the burning trunks, even the embers, to the Indians posted at their stations along the way back to the village. The Indians were so thorough, not even an ember was left behind. Nothing was left for the Jaguar.

That evening, Botoque's village celebrated the end of cold darkness at night. They grilled fresh meat to share with all the villagers, and danced and slept by the warmth of the fire.

When the Jaguar returned home, his sweetness and generosity were twisted into anger. He felt betrayed by his stepson. He had openly shared with Botoque the secret of the bow and arrow, and he assumed the boy would tell the villagers. Yet the trusting Jaguar never suspected that his adopted son would steal the fire. The old Jaguar was so incensed by the ingratitude of Botoque, he suddenly transformed from the civilized creature he had always been into a ferocious animal. The vine he tied around his waist when he went hunting sprouted into a tail. Fur grew all over his body, and he could only walk on all fours.

As night wore on, the Jaguar began to feel the cold. Without the fire, he would need his new fur to keep warm. His anger escalated. He raged up and exclaimed, "If this is the way the Indians want it to be, from now on I will devour them. I will hunt in the dark. I will feel the cold, and when I encounter the Indians, I will eat them raw."

All that remains of the fire for the Jaguar is his remembrance of it and to this day, that memory shines in his eyes. Once so civilized, the Jaguar now hunts with his fangs and eats only raw meat. The Jaguar's good and civilized spirit was corrupted by Botoque's betrayal, and the mighty Jaguar trusts no one.

COMMENT: *The story of Botoque and the Jaguar is told in many of the tribes of the Brazilian Indians. At the start of this tale, the Jaguar was more civilized in his ways than the Indian. He had possession of fire, knew about eating cooked meat, and was able to hunt for his prey with ease by using the bow and arrow. He stood erect, his body was not covered with fur, and he could talk. The Indians at that time knew only darkness and cold at night, ate their meat raw, and hunted with spears and rocks.*

The Indians' acceptance of animals as equal or better than

themselves is illustrated by the Jaguar's relationship with Botoque. He saves Botoque, adopts him as a son, and shows the boy a new weapon and the existence of fire.

When his fire is stolen, the Jaguar abandons his civilized ways in order to retaliate against the human race which has betrayed him. The jaguar is the most feared animal of the rain forest, and the Indians use this myth to explain the origin of the jaguar's ferocity which sets him apart from the other animals.

Glossary

AÇAÍ PALM	Type of palm tree (*Euterpe oleracea*).
ACURANA	Type of night owl.
AGOUTI	Slender–limbed rodent about the size of a rabbit (*Dasyprocta agouti*).
ANACONDA	Large serpent that can grow to 40 feet. It weighs more than 300 pounds and crushes its prey in its coils (*Eunectes murinus*).
ANNATTO SEEDS	Seeds of the annatto tree which produce a red dye the Indians use to decorate their bodies and their artifacts (*Bixa orellana*). Annatto is called *urucu* by the Amazonian Indians.
ARMADILLO	Burrowing mammal having an armor–like covering of jointed plates (fam. *Dasipodideos*).
BEIJU	Flat cake made of manioc flour.
CALABASH	Hard–shelled gourd–like fruit from the calabash tree (*Lagenaria Siceraria*) used for making vessels.

CAPYBARA   Edible, South American rodent, that can grow up to four feet long (*Hydrochoerus capybara*).

CASHEW   Edible nut bearing tree that is aboriginal to Brazil (*Anacardium occidentale*).

CASSAVA   Shrub cultivated for its edible root. Also called manioc or mandioc (genus *Manihot*).

CAXIRI   Alcoholic beverage made of fermented manioc juice.

COCKATOO   Brightly colored crested parrot (*Kakatoë*).

COROLLA   Inner circle of flower petals.

CURASSOW   A large, turkey–like bird, called *mutum* by the Indians (fam. *Crasidae*).

CURARE   A resinous extract of certain South American trees, especially *Strychnos toxifera* and *Chondrodrendon tomentosum*, that, when introduced into the blood stream, paralyzes the motor nerves. It is used as an arrow poison, to reduce muscular spasms, and in general anesthesia.

EGRET   Heron–like bird (*Casmerodius albus*).

EMU   Flightless large bird related to the ostrich (genus *Dromiceius*).

FICUS   Fig tree (*Ficus*).

GENIPAPO   Tree whose seeds produce a black dye which the Indians use to decorate their bodies and their artifacts (*Genipa americana*).

GUARANÁ   Shrub whose seeds are used for medicinal purposes (*Paulinia sorbilis*).

GUAVA   Pear–shaped edible fruit (genus *Psidium*).

IBIS   Wading bird related to the heron (fam. *Threskiornithidae*).

ICAMIABAS   Legendary tribe of moon–worshiping Indian warrior women who lived without men and did not allow any other tribe to approach them.

IGARAPÉ   Narrow riverbank between two islands or between an island and the mainland. Stream or rivulet.

JACARANDA   Tropical American tree (genus *Jacaranda*).

JATOBÁ   A large tropical tree. Its bark is often used in making canoes (*Hymenaea courbaril*).

JURUTAI   A bird of the Caprimulgidae family (*Nyctibus grandis*).

LIANA   Any of various climbing plants of tropical forests with ropelike dangling stems and roots.

MACAW   Large tropical parrot with long tail, harsh voice, and brilliant plumage (genus *Ara*).

MADEIRA RIVER   River in Brazil. Tributary of the Amazon River.

MAIZE   Corn (*Zea mays*).

MARACUJÁ	Passion fruit. Edible fruit from the passion flower shrub, believed to have sedative qualities (genus *Passiflora*).
MALOCA	Indian communal hut shared by several families.
MANAKIN	A tropical American bird of brilliant plumage (fam. *Pripidae*).
MANIOC	Also called mandioc or mandióca; cassava tuber plant with edible roots (genus *Manihot*).
MATÉ	A tea made from the leaves of a Brazilian holly (*Ilex paraguariensis*) used as a beverage in South America.
MIMOSA FLOWER	Small, fragrant yellow flower of the tropical mimosa tree (genus *Mimosa*).
MIRITI	Palm tree whose fronds are used for basketry. The fruit of the *miriti* palm is used for making oil, wine, and flour (*Mauritia flexuosa*).
MORPHO	Large butterfly with blue–black wings.
MURUCUTUTÚ	Owl–like nocturnal bird.
PACA	Large, semi–nocturnal rodent, brown with white spots (*Coelogenys paca*).
PAPAYA	Yellow melon–like fruit of a tropical American tree (*Carica papaya*).
PECCARY	Several species of wild boar of the genus *Tayassu*.

PEQUÍ TREE	Large tree that can measure up to 15 feet in diameter at the base. The fruit of the *pequí* is edible and used for making oil.
PIAVA	A small freshwater fish.
PINTADO	A freshwater fish.
PIRARUCU	Largest of freshwater fish found in the Amazon region. Can be over 6 feet long and weigh 250 pounds or more (*Arapium gigas*).
PIRANHA	Small, voracious freshwater fish with massive jaws and sharp teeth (genus *Serosalmo*).
PUMA	Carnivore of the cat family; mountain cat; cougar (*Felis concolor*).
PUPUNHA PALM	Type of palm tree that bears edible nuts (*Guilielma speciosa*).
SHAMAN	Tribal medicine man and interpreter of the spirits. Spiritual leader of the tribe.
SNIPE	Long–billed shore or marsh bird (*Gallinago*).
SPOONBILL	Pink wading bird related to the ibis. Has a broad or flattened bill (genus *Platalea*).
TAPAJÓS RIVER	River in Brazil. A tributary of the Amazon river.
TAPIR	Large nocturnal mammal that grows to be 3 feet high. The tapir has short, stout limbs and a flexible snout (fam. *Tapiridae*).

TARO	Tropical plant of the *Arum* family grown for its edible cornlike rootstocks (genus *Colocasia*).
TIMBÓ	Woody vines used by the Indians for capturing fish, which, when crushed and immersed in the water, release a poison that kills the fish by paralyzing their breathing. The fish can then be easily speared or gathered in nets (*Tephrosia, Lonchocarpus, Derris*).
TOCANTINS RIVER	River in the Northeast part of Brazil.
TOUCAN	Large fruit-eating bird with brilliant plumage and an immense beak (fam. *Rhamphastidae*).
TUCUMÃ TREE	Type of palm tree (*Astrocayurm* sp.).
UBÁ	Canoe made from the whole bark of a single tree.
URUCU	Annatto plant whose seeds produce a red dye used by the Indians for body painting and food coloring (*Bixa orellana*).
VICTORIA REGIA	Giant water lily (*Victoria regia*).

Credits

FOR THE TALES

(See bibliography for complete copyright information)

THE FIRST PEOPLE

Mindlin, Betty. "História do Começo do Mundo" narrated by Konkuat, from *Tuparis e Tapurás*.

Osborne, Harold. "The Origins of Man" documented by Franz Caspar from *South American Mythology*.

Wilbert, Johannes and Karin Simoneau. "The Hole in the Sky" documented by Lukesch and "The Men from the Sky" documented by Banner from *Folk Literature of the Ge Indians*.

THE CREATION OF NIGHT

Gerson, Mary Joan. *How Night Came from the Sea. A Story from Brazil*.

Kuss, Daniel and Jean Torton. "Donde vem a Noite?" from *A Amazônia: Mitos e Lendas*.

Lippert, Margaret H. *The Sea Serpent's Daughter. A Brazilian Legend*.

Oliveira, José Coutinho de. "Como se fez a Noite" from *Folclore Amazônico*.

Santos, Theobaldo Miranda. "A Criação da Noite" from *Lendas e Mitos do Brasil*.

THE ORIGIN OF RAIN AND THUNDER

Azulgaray, Domingo and Catia, ed. *Brasil, Histórias, Costumes e Lendas*.

Lévi–Strauss, Claude. "The Origin of Rain and Storms" documented by Lukesch and Banner, from *The Raw and the Cooked*.

Schultz, Harald. *Hombú, Indian Life in the Brazilian Jungle*.

Wilbert, Johannes and Karin Simoneau. "The Man who turned into Rain," documented by Lukesch; "The Man of the Rain" documented by Banner; and "The Origin of Rain and Thunder" documented by Métraux, from *Folk Literature of the Ge Indians*.

HOW THE STARS CAME TO BE

Fittipaldi, Ciça. *Subida Pro Céu. Mito dos Índios Bororo*.

Lévi–Strauss, Claude. "The Origin of the Stars" documented by Colbacchini, from *The Raw and the Cooked*.

Santos, Theobaldo Miranda. "A Origem das Estrelas" from *Lendas e Mitos do Brasil*.

Wilbert, Johannes and Karin Simoneau. "The Origin of the Stars and of Certain Animals" documented by Albisetti and Venturelli and "The Hole in the Sky" documented by Lukesch, from *Folk Literature of the Bororo Indians*.

THE LEGEND OF THE YARA

Bettencourt, Gastão de. "A Iara," by Bilac; Olegário Mariano's poem based on a tale by Affonso Arinhos; "Clan do Jaboti" by Mario de Andrade. All from *A Amazônia no Fabulario e na Arte*.

Bezerra, Ararê Marrocos and Ana Maria T. de Paula. "Oiara" from *Lendas e Mitos da Amazônia*.

De Onis, Harriet. "The Yara" by Affonso Arinhos de Melo Franco from *The Golden Land: An Anthology of Latin American Folklore in Literature*.

Santos, Theobaldo Miranda. "A Sedução da Iara" from *Lendas e Mitos do Brasil*.

UNIAÍ'S SON AND THE GUARANÁ

Cruls, Gastão. "Noticia Sobre o Uaraná" by Silva Coutinho from *Hiléia Amazônica*.

Bezerra, Ararê Marrocos and Ana Maria T. De Paula. *Lendas e Mitos da Amazônia*.

Fittipaldi, Ciça. *A Lenda do Guaraná: Mito dos Índios Sateré-Maué*.

Oliveira, José Coutinho de. "O Guaraná" from *Folclore Amazônico*.

Santos, Theobaldo Miranda. "Os Olhos do Menino" from *Lendas e Mitos do Brasil*.

THE VICTORIA REGIA

Bettencourt, Gastão de. "Terra Imatura" by Alfredo Ladislau from *A Amazônia no Fabulario e na Arte*.

Cruls, Gastão. *Hiléia Amazônica*.

Santos, Theobaldo Miranda. "A Vitória-Régia" from *Lendas e Mitos do Brasil*.

THE ORIGIN OF BIRDS, PLANTS,
AND SOIL TERMITES

Fittipaldi, Ciça. *O Menino e a Flauta: Mito dos Índios Nambiquara*.

Wilbert, Johannes and Karin Simoneau. "How the Birds and the Soil Termites Were Made," documented by Oliveira *Folk Literature of the Ge Indians*.

THE YOUNG MAN AND THE STAR MAIDEN

Bierhorst, John. *The Mythology of South America*.

Elbl, Martin. "The Man who Married a Star" from *Tales from the Amazon*.

Frost, Frances. "Rairu and the Star Maiden" from *Legends of the United Nations*.

Giaccaria, Bartolomeu and Alberto Heide. "O Rapaz e a Estrela" from *Jeronimo Xavante Conta: Mitos e Lendas*.

Kuss, Daniel and Jean Torton. "Dénakê e a Grande Estrela" from *A Amazônia. Mitos e Lendas*.

Lévi-Strauss, Claude. "The Origin of Cultivated Plants" documented from different tribes by Nimuendaju, Schultz, and Banner from *The Raw and the Cooked*.

BOTOQUE, THE JAGUAR AND THE FIRE

Bierhorst, John. *The Mythology of South America.*

Giaccaria, Bartolomeu and Alberto Heide. "O Rapaz, a Onça e o Fogo" from *Jeronimo Xavante Conta: Mitos e Lendas.*

Lévi–Strauss, Claude. "The origin of fire" documented from different tribes by Banner, Nimuendaju, and Métraux from *The Raw and the Cooked.*

Wilbert, Johannes and Karin Simoneau. "The Fire and the Jaguar" documented by Banner from *Folk Literature of the Ge Indians.*

List of Illustrations

Every effort has been made to locate the copyright owners of the illustrations and sources reproduced in this book. Omissions brought to our attention will be corrected in subsequent editions.

Bibliography

Alzugaray, Domingo & Catia, ed. *Brasil, Histórias, Costumes, e Lendas.* São Paulo: Editora Tres, 1993.

Basso, Ellen B. *In Favor of Deceit: A Study of Tricksters in an Amazon Society.* Tucson: University of Arizona Press, 1978.

Bates, Henry Walter. *O Naturalista no Rio Amazonas.* São Paulo: Companhia Editora Nacional, 1944.

Belluzo, Ana Maria de Moraes. *O Brazil dos Viagantes. Imaginario do Novo Mundo.* Vol. I. São Paulo: Metalivros, 1994.

Bettencourt, Gastão de. *A Amazônia no Fabulario e na Arte.* Lisboa: Pro Domo, 1946.

Bezerra, Ararê Marrocos and Ana Maria T. De Paula. *Lendas e Mitos da Amazônia.* Belém: Embratel, Demec/PA, 1985.

Bierhorst, John. *The Mythology of South America.* New York: Quill, 1988.

Boggs, Ralph Steele. *Bibliography of Latin American Folklore.* Detroit, 1971.

Brasil, Altino Berthier. *O Tuxáua Buope e Seu Império Amazônico. Lendas do Rio Negro e do Uaupés.* Porto Alegre: Editora Movimento, 1982.

Cascudo, Luis da Camara. *Geografia dos Mitos Brasileiros.* Belo Horizonte: Editora Itatiaia Ltda., 1983.

Cruls, Gastão. *Hiléia Amazônica.* Rio de Janeiro: José Olympio, 1958.

Cunha, Manuela Carneiro da. *História dos Índios no Brasil.* São Paulo: Companhia das Letras, 1992.

De Onis, Harriet. *The Golden Land: An Anthology of Latin American Folklore in Literature.* New York: Alfred Knopf, 1966. First published in 1948.

Debret, Jean Baptiste. *Viagem Pitoresca e Histórica ao Brasil.* Belo Horizonte: Editora Itatiaia, 1989.

Denslow, Julie Sloan and Christine Padoch. *People of the Tropical Rainforest.* Berkeley: University of California Press, 1988.

Descola, Philippe. *The Spears of Twilight: Life and Death in the Amazon Jungle.* New York: The New Press, 1996.

Elbl, Martin. *Tales from the Amazon.* Burlington, Ontario: Hayes Publishing Ltd., 1986.

Fittipaldi, Ciça. *O Menino e a Flauta: Mito dos Índios Nambiquara.* São Paulo: Melhoramentos, 1986.

——. *Subida Pro Céu: Mito dos Índios Bororo.* São Paulo: Melhoramentos, 1986.

——. *A Lenda do Guaraná: Mito dos Índios Sateré-Maué.* São Paulo: Melhoramentos, 1986.

Flora. *Feathers Like a Rainbow.* New York: HarperCollins, 1989.

Florence, Hercules. *A Descoberta da Amazônia.* São Paulo: Editora Marca D'Agua, 1995.

Frost, Frances. *Legends of the United Nations.* New York: McGraw Hill, 1943.

Gerson, Mary Joan. *How Night Came from the Sea: A Story from Brazil.* Toronto: Little, Brown and Co., 1994.

Gheerbrant, Alain. *The Amazon, Past, Present and Future.* New York: Harry N. Abrams, 1992.

Giaccaria, Bartolomeu and Alberto Heide. *Jeronimo Xavante Conta: Mitos e Lendas.* Campo Grande: Casa da Cultura, 1975.

Kuss, Daniel and Jean Torton. *A Amazônia: Mitos e Lendas.* Amadora: Bertrand Editora, 1991.

Lévi-Strauss, Claude. *The Raw and the Cooked.* Chicago: University of Chicago Press, 1983.

Lippert, Margaret H. *The Sea Serpent's Daughter. A Brazilian Legend.* Mahwah, NJ: Troll Associates, 1993.

Mendes, Amando. *Vocabulario Amazônico.* São Paulo: Sociedade Impressora Brasileira, 1942.

Mindlin, Betty. *Tuparis e Tapurás.* São Paulo: Editora Brasiliense, 1993.

Mindlin, Betty and Fernando Portela. *A Questão do Índio.* São Paulo: Editora Atica, 1995.

Oliveira, José Coutinho de. *Folclore Amazônico.* Belém: Editora São José, 1951.

Osborne, Harold. *South American Mythology.* Feltham: Hamlyn Publishing Group, 1968.

Rocha, Ana Augusta and Roberto Linsker. *Brasil Aventura.* São Paulo: Terra Virgem, 1995.

Santos, Theobaldo Miranda. *Lendas e Mitos do Brasil.* São Paulo: Editora Nacional, 1992.

Schultz, Harald. *Hombú, Indian Life in the Brazilian Jungle.* New York: MacMillan Co., 1962.

Seward, Julian H., ed. *The Handbook of South American Indians.* Vol. III. Washington, D.C.: U.S. Government Printing Office, 1948.

Souza Aranha, Maria Amélia Arruda Botelho. *Lendas de Amor do Folclore Indígena.* São Paulo: Livraria Martins, 1964.

Villas Bôas, Orlando and Claudio. *Xingú: The Indians, Their Myths.* New York: Farrar, Straus, Giroux, 1973.

—— and Maureen Bisilliat. *Xingú, Territorio Tribal.* São Paulo: Cultura Editores Associados, 1990.

Wilbert, Johannes, and Karin Simoneau. *Folk Literature of the Ge Indians.* Los Angeles: U.C.L.A. Latin American Center Publications, 1978.

——. *Folk Literature of the Bororo Indians.* Los Angeles: U.C.L.A. Latin American Center Publications, 1983.

——. *Folk Literature of the Yanomami Indians.* Los Angeles: U.C.L.A. Latin American Center Publications, 1990.

About the Editors

MERCEDES DORSON was born and raised in Brazil. She has traveled in the Amazon region and spent time among the Brazilian Indians. Currently she lives with her husband and two children in New York City.

JEANNE WILMOT is the author of *Dirt Angel*, a collection of short stories published this year. Her prize-winning work has appeared in numerous publications, as well as in the *O. Henry Stories*. She is an attorney and Associate Publisher of The Ecco Press and lives with her husband and daughter in Princeton, New Jersey.